"Camille is going to hit you hard, Pike.

She's going to tell the jury you operate on the basis of personal revenge. She'll say you're still trying to get even for your wife's death. She'll accuse you of bias and prejudice. And if she's successful, the jury won't have much confidence in what you've told them."

Looking at the assistant district attorney, Pike uttered an oath. "Camille wouldn't stoop to that."

"Why not? It happens all the time. Defense lawyers are fighting for their clients. They'll stop at nothing."

"Camille isn't like that," he insisted.

"You sound like you're carrying a torch for her. Don't let your feelings interfere with your thinking, Pike."

Pike sat in stony silence, torn by conflicting emotions. Camille had aroused tender feelings he didn't want to have. Now he was hearing that she'd be a tough, ruthless adversary who'd grab hold of the most painful episode in his life and squeeze it. She knew his weak spot. Would she torture him by using it?

Dear Reader,

Welcome to the Silhouette **Special Edition** experience! With your search for consistently satisfying reading in mind, every month the authors and editors of Silhouette **Special Edition** aim to offer you a stimulating blend of deep emotions and high romance.

The name Silhouette **Special Edition** and the distinctive arch on the cover represent a commitment—a commitment to bring you six sensitive, substantial novels each month. In the pages of a Silhouette **Special Edition**, compelling true-to-life characters face riveting emotional issues—and come out winners. All the authors in the series strive for depth, vividness and warmth in writing these stories of living and loving in today's world.

The result, we hope, is romance you can believe in. Deeply emotional, richly romantic, infinitely rewarding—that's the Silhouette **Special Edition** experience. Come share it with us—six times a month!

From all the authors and editors of Silhouette **Special Edition**,

Best wishes,

Leslie Kazanjian,
Senior Editor

KATE MERIWETHER
Petticoat Lawyer

Silhouette Special Edition

Published by Silhouette Books New York

America's Publisher of Contemporary Romance

KATE MERIWETHER

is a practicing attorney and lives in Texas. Since she was a young girl, she has loved reading romances, and it was her lifetime dream to write romances that other readers would enjoy.

Chapter One

Camille Clark made her way through the tangled clusters of people waiting for the afternoon session of court in Travis County to begin.

"Over here," signaled the bailiff. "We're holding your client in an empty jury room so you can talk to her before the judge calls her case."

"Thanks." Camille glanced at her watch. The judge's secretary had called only half an hour ago to notify her that she'd been court-appointed to a new case. Camille would be lucky to have five minutes alone with her client before arraignments began. Frowning, she brushed her short blond hair back from her forehead and followed Bailiff Seales at a fast clip, her high heels clicking on the marble floor.

She felt heads turn as she passed other lawyers, the courthouse regulars, and wondered what they were thinking. She hated it when they speculated about why her marriage to a rising young criminal attorney had fallen apart last year. She hated it even worse when they speculated about whether she was going to be able to put her own career back together. Well, she'd worked hard to rid herself of the soft, feminine traits that had sabotaged everything. Maybe today they were noticing her new image, the padded shoulders and short, slim skirt that marked her as sassy and sophisticated. No more lace-trimmed blouses, no more shoulder-length blond waves. Camille squared her chin. Look sassy and sophisticated, she reminded herself, but act *tough*. And don't let your guard down for a minute.

Bailiff Seales stopped at the door of the jury room and knocked briskly.

"Yeah?" challenged an unseen male from inside the jury room.

"The defendant's lawyer is here." The bailiff opened the door and ushered Camille inside without waiting for permission. The cops might run things down at the police station, but the courthouse was *his* territory.

Camille glanced past the bailiff and saw Lieutenant Pike Barrett from the special crimes unit sprawled scowl-faced near her handcuffed client, Jenny Mayner. Camille knew Pike by sight, as he did her, though they'd never worked on the same case before. She'd always thought he was attractive in an offbeat sort of way. Not her type; too serious and probably cantankerous judging from his frown.

"What's happened?" Camille pondered as Jenny dropped her head, too ashamed to meet Camille's eyes. Camille had represented Jenny in the past when she'd been hauled into juvenile court for running away from home, but Jenny had never committed any kind of violent crime before. So what had put her in the custody of Pike Barrett, top dog of the special crimes unit? He was known as a good cop, and he wouldn't be here with Jenny if something terrible hadn't happened.

There was no time now to sort out her conflicting emotions at the sight of Jenny, red-eyed from weeping. Camille would have to respond with the trained instincts of a professional and make the most of the precious little time she'd been granted with her client.

"I'd like to speak with my client alone." Her tone insisted rather than requested.

Pike Barrett shrugged and pushed himself away from the time-bitten jury table. He seemed taller, lankier than Camille remembered from past encounters at the courthouse. His hair and eyes appeared darker, almost menacing in the shadows cast by the bare light bulb high overhead. He was known in the legal community as a fair cop, but exasperatingly thorough. Every *i* had to be dotted, every *t* crossed. He played by the rules and demanded the same from everyone else. No inside information to courthouse favorites, no tips on weak spots in the district attorney's case, no special favors to anyone.

Camille felt her stomach tighten in a knot of anxiety. She'd taken an oath to do her best for any client charged with a crime. She'd never defended a case involving Pike Barrett before, but she knew his reputation. What serious crime was Jenny being charged with? And how much did Pike Barrett know about the circumstances?

"The handcuffs?" Camille asked.

Pike shot her an irritated look, then leaned over and unlocked the cuffs that bound Jenny's wrists. "Guess it's okay," he conceded. "She was searched at the station before we brought her over here."

Jenny Mayner continued to sit with her head down, her long, taffy-colored hair falling over her face to hide her eyes. Camille stood waiting until Pike unfastened the cuffs and left the room, then closed the door with a slight rasping noise.

"We haven't got much time, Jenny." Camille sat down and drew a yellow legal pad from her briefcase. "Tell me what happened."

"I don't have anything to say." Jenny's voice was muffled, full of anger and self-pity.

There wasn't time to waste trying to coax her to talk. Camille picked up the file Pike Barrett had left on the jury table and flipped it open to the offense report made at the time of Jenny's arrest. Reading quickly, she absorbed the information and tried not to reveal her dismay. It looked like an open-and-shut case, almost as though Jenny had *wanted* to get caught committing a crime. When she finished reading, she turned to Jenny with a grim expression. "Okay, talk fast, Jenny, because we don't have much time. What made you commit an armed robbery in full view of a cruising squad car?"

Jenny's head slumped even lower. "I told you, I don't want to talk about it."

"I'm your lawyer, Jenny. I can't help you unless you cooperate with me."

Jenny stubbornly turned her head and stared at a crack in the plaster.

"This is a serious charge, Jenny. And you're not a juvenile anymore. The juvenile code only protects kids between ten and seventeen. You're past seventeen now. That means you'll be tried as an adult. A jury could give you ninety-nine years for armed robbery."

A frantic look passed momentarily over Jenny's face, and she seemed to be on the verge of blurting out a response. Then just as quickly she changed her mind. "I don't want a lawyer. I can't afford one, anyway."

"I'm court-appointed, Jenny. The judge remembered that I represented you before when you were a juvenile. Travis County will pay me to defend your case." Though Camille might well donate legal services worth thousands of dollars to Jenny's defense, she didn't mention that the standard fee paid by the county was less than three hundred dollars. Even that would sound like a fortune to a girl like Jenny. Besides, Camille felt very strongly that it was her personal and professional obligation to help people who couldn't afford a lawyer. "It won't cost you anything since you're what they call indigent."

"What does that mean?" Jenny hunched in her chair, scarcely curious about the courthouse proceedings swirling around her.

"That you can't afford to pay a lawyer. It's the truth, isn't it?"

"I don't want a lawyer. I just want to enter a guilty plea and get it over with."

"It's much too soon to decide how to handle your case, Jenny. First I have to do some investigation and see everything the D.A. has on you. We can decide later about whether to go to trial."

There seemed to be panic in Jenny's voice. "No! There's not going to be any trial."

"Is your mother coming for the arraignment today?" Camille asked, changing the subject in an effort to calm Jenny down.

Jenny shook her head. "I told her to stay away. She can't handle things like this."

"I'm sure it's hard for a mother to watch her child in court, but you need her emotional support, Jenny."

"Leave my mom out of this! It's my problem. I can handle it by myself."

Sure you can, Camille thought, but there was no point in arguing. She'd forgotten how stubborn Jenny could be.

There was a knock at the door. "Judge is ready to start calling the arraignments, Ms. Clark."

"I need a few more minutes."

"Sorry." Bailiff Seales opened the door and fumbled for the handcuffs, then secured them over Jenny's slender wrists. "We can take these off when you're at the counsel table," he explained, "but you have to wear them while you're being moved through the corridors. It's standard courthouse procedure." He took Jenny firmly in tow and headed toward the courtroom, Camille following a half step behind.

Camille veered aside to speak to Pike Barrett, looking mismatched in civilian clothes as he stood with a group of police officers in navy-blue uniforms. The rumpled khaki suit gave him the disheveled attractiveness of a private-eye hero in a television movie. If he'd just smile, he might be downright good-looking. But he didn't look as though he'd had much practice with smiling. His lips looked starched and ironed in a rigid line. No use wasting her charm on someone who was so disagreeable. "You could've mentioned that you were the arresting officer."

A ridge formed between his nose and mouth as he scowled, trying to take her measure and seeming unsure of the result. "No need," he said, his words a little too slow, a little too soft. "You were bound to find it in the offense report."

"I can't get Jenny to talk to me about the robbery. Did she say anything when you arrested her?"

"You saw my report. Anything else you've got to get from the D.A." Pike turned aside to rejoin the group of police officers.

Stung by his dismissal, Camille felt her self-confidence drain right out of her. How many times had her ex-husband turned his back on her and made her feel either stupid or rejected, just as she did right now? Camille tightened her fists and felt her long, bright red nails dig into her palms. The pain was just the reminder she needed. Bright red nails. Bright red lipstick. Broad shoulders. Short skirts. Sassy. Sophisticated. *Tough*.

She gave Pike a chilly smile as she detoured around his group and went into the courtroom. This fight is only beginning, she thought as she seated herself and waited for Jenny's name to be called. Camille had a lot to prove to herself, and she would begin with Lieutenant Pike Barrett.

Camille sat beside her client at the counsel table in the middle of the old-fashioned courtroom, watching while Judge Michelsohn made notes on his docket sheet as he went through the routine of Jenny Mayner's arraignment: attorney appointed, charges read, plea taken, trial date set. "What is the prosecutor's recommended amount for bail?" he asked in his usual soft-spoken drawl. He'd been on the bench for many years and never seemed to be in any hurry.

"The State requests that the defendant post bail of fifty thousand dollars, your honor." Dorcas Wilson, an assistant district attorney, stood with a file in her hand and waited for the protest that inevitably came when the prosecutor requested a high bail.

Camille was already on her feet. "Your Honor, fifty thousand dollars is clearly excessive. This is a first offense, and my client is a seventeen-year-old schoolgirl. She couldn't raise fifteen thousand dollars' bail, let alone fifty thousand."

"This is *not* a first offense, your Honor." Dorcas adjusted the oversized frames of her glasses so they fit properly on the bridge of her pert nose. "The defendant has been in court on a number of occasions in the past. She was a chronic runaway as a juvenile, so her bail needs to be high enough to keep her from running away again."

"Juvenile records are sealed and cannot be used in a subsequent criminal case after the child turns seventeen. The court knows that if the prosecutor doesn't." Camille let her anger show. Maybe Dorcas Wilson, a recent addition to the district attorney's staff, could be intimidated into making another mistake.

"Now, now, counsel, this is only an arraignment, not a jury trial." The judge waved Camille back into her seat at the counsel table. "Ms. Wilson, do you have independent testimony about the defendant's likelihood of fleeing the jurisdiction of this court prior to trial? Other than the juvenile court records, I mean."

Dorcas signaled to Pike and whispered something in his ear as he leaned toward her, then nodded.

"Lieutenant Barrett will testify if the court wishes."

Pike went forward to be sworn, then took the stand and answered the standard questions about his employment as a police officer and his acquaintance with the defendant, Jenny Mayner. To Camille's surprise, Pike had previously been assigned to Jenny's East Austin neighborhood and remembered her as an unhappy teen from a poor single-parent family.

"Jenny's mother just never could seem to make it after her husband died," he explained. "She had trouble getting a job, and when she did get one, it never seemed to last long."

Jenny tugged at Camille's sleeve. "Make him stop talking about my mom," she demanded, her face pinched and drawn.

"I need to find out what he knows about you, Jenny. This is a good way to test the waters and see what kind of witness he'll be at trial. This won't hurt your case because there's no jury present to hear him."

"What do you know about what's going to hurt my case? You don't know anything about it. Make him be quiet, I tell you. I'm not going to have him talking about me and my family in front of all these people." Jenny waved at the courtroom half-full of lawyers and criminal defendants waiting their turn to be called, all listening curiously because there was nothing better to do in the meantime.

"I know it's embarrassing for you. I'm sorry. But it's better for you to be embarrassed for ten minutes now than to spend thirty or forty years in prison for armed robbery. I need your cooperation, Jenny, and I expect you to give it to me." Though her words were whispered, Camille said them in dead earnest.

She might as well have been speaking Swahili, though, because Jenny suddenly stood and pushed aside her chair.

"That's enough! Take me back to jail. I don't care if you set my bail at a million dollars!" Jenny's face reddened, then crumpled as angry tears streamed down her cheeks. "I'm the one that's been arrested, not my family!"

The bailiff rushed over to Jenny and got her back in her seat, then pulled handcuffs from his hip pocket but quickly replaced them at a negative gesture from the judge. The spectators in the courtroom riveted their attention on the novel scene that was unfolding. They, too, glanced toward the judge and wondered what would happen next.

Judge Michelsohn retained his unflappable demeanor and instructed the bailiff to give Jenny a drink of water, then waited until she'd gotten her jerky breathing under control again.

"I'm sorry if our courtroom routine distresses you," he said firmly. "But we're here to get valid information so we can make the right decisions and see that justice is done. It's important for me to know as much about you as possible so I can be fair when I set the amount of your bail. The Constitution requires me to protect your rights as well as those of the citizens of Travis County. I hope you appreciate what a difficult job that can be for a judge.''

He gave Jenny a stern look but she paid no attention. She was too wrapped up in her own problems to listen to a civics lecture. He turned his attention to Camille. ''Do you wish to cross-examine this witness?''

Camille gave Pike a studied gaze. He was the arresting officer as well as eyewitness to an armed robbery that so far Camille knew very little about. Pike knew something of her client's history over a period of several years. He knew the prosecutor wanted fifty thousand dollars' bail. He probably wanted the bail set at least that high himself. He knew Jenny had been a runaway. All good reasons to let him off the stand without cross-examination, all good reasons why he'd probably recommend a high bail for Jenny. But if Camille let him go without asking a single question, she'd look weak and scared of his testimony. She had to look strong now in order to help Jenny's case later. But how? What trait did he have that Camille could appeal to, use to an advantage? She quickly prodded her memory for details about Pike's reputation, but all she remembered was his reputation for being fair and playing by the rules.

She took a deep breath and stared into his eyes. ''Lieutenant Barrett, you've already told the court all the reasons why my client should have a *high* bail.

Now will you tell the court all the reasons why a *lower* bail might be appropriate?''

Dorcas Wilson was on her feet shouting an objection, but the judge overruled her and tried to hide an ironic smile as he waited for Pike's answer.

Pike squirmed in the witness seat, but not once did he avert his eyes from Camille's stare. "As far as I know, Jenny hasn't been in any trouble for the past year. After that last runaway charge, she got herself back in school and took a part-time job." He paused, trying to remember everything he could. "I don't see her hanging around with a bad crowd when I cruise the east side these days." He shrugged. "I guess that's about it."

"Thank you. No more questions." Camille felt a rush of elation. He'd given testimony that would make Jenny look a little better in the judge's eyes. Maybe there was still a chance for minimum bail.

Judge Michelsohn waved Pike back into his seat before he could leave the stand. "One thing I'd like to know, Lieutenant Barrett. What amount of bail do *you* think would be fair to this defendant and to the citizens of Travis County?"

Pike expelled his breath with a soft whoosh, obviously relieved to have a chance to qualify the answer he'd just given Camille. "Well, your Honor, the defendant is charged with armed robbery. That's one of the most serious crimes there is. Even if you allow for her being young and impulsive, or even stupid, and give her full credit for putting her life back together, she's still charged with a violent crime. An innocent bystander could've gotten killed with that loaded revolver she was waving around. Personally I don't think fifty thousand dollars' bail is all that unreasonable." Slowly Pike shook his head, as though shaking away a dream, then added in a tight voice. "But to be absolutely fair, I guess I'd recommend bail of twenty-five thousand."

"Twenty-five thousand it is." The judge made a note on the docket sheet. "Thank you, Lieutenant Barrett. You can step down from the witness stand." He put Jenny's court file in a stack and picked up the next one. "Bailiff, see that the defendant Jenny Mayner is kept in custody until such time as she posts twenty-five thousand dollars' bail. Her trial is set for January seventh."

As the judge called the next case, there was a rapid rotation of lawyers and defendants. Camille found herself in the corridor outside while the bailiff fastened Jenny's handcuffs. "I don't suppose you'll be able to post bail?"

Jenny shook her head. They both knew it meant she would have to stay in jail until the time of her trial, nearly two months from now. It was a bleak prospect for a seventeen-year-old girl.

"I'll come to see you in a day or two and start putting together your case. In the meantime, don't talk to anybody about it—not the other prisoners, not the guards, nobody. Understand? Anything you say to anybody can be used against you at trial." When

Jenny stared into space, oblivious to her instructions, Camille grew exasperated. "This is important, Jenny, so listen up! You're going to have to do exactly what I tell you or I can't help you, damn it!"

"You can't help me anyway. It's too late for that. Nobody can help me."

Anger and frustration made Camille grip Jenny's upper arm and give it a shake. "Don't you dare give up on yourself, Jenny Mayner! And don't think it's too late for anybody to help you. This is still America, and you're still presumed innocent until proven guilty in a court of law! You do your part and I'll do mine, you can count on that."

Jenny turned silent and unheeding to follow the bailiff.

"Don't throw away your life, you little fool!" Camille murmured into the empty air. Then she went to find Pike Barrett.

The wary expression in Pike's eyes told Camille he wasn't exactly pleased about having to carry on another conversation with her. One of the blue-uniformed officers made a joshing remark as Pike departed their group. The lines were clearly drawn, cops versus defense lawyers. Pike had his place on one side of the line, with Camille on the other. Yet in a public courtroom she had managed to drag him across the line with one well-phrased question. His uniformed buddies had been among the spectators when Pike had to testify in support of lowered bail for Jenny, and

Camille realized she'd put him on the spot in front of his peers. Right now she didn't care what *they* thought, but it was important to get some cooperation from Pike. "Can we go in the jury room for a few minutes?" she asked, knowing she needed to get him out of earshot of the other cops.

"Look, I told you to talk with the district attorney. Everything I have to say is in my report."

"Dorcas will be tied up in the courtroom for another hour finishing up all those arraignments. I'll be happy to wait for her, though, if you'll wait, too." Camille gave him one of those bright smiles that didn't quite reach her eyes. She knew how cops felt about hanging around the courthouse; this guy wanted out of here.

He glanced at his watch. "I was supposed to go off duty at three o'clock."

She shrugged. "I guess I could come by the police station tomorrow and interview you there."

She almost felt him wince. That was all he needed, said his dour expression. It would be all over the station that he was getting chummy with a criminal defense lawyer. Without another word he shoved his fists into his pockets and stalked across the corridor to an unused jury room. Camille could hardly keep up with his long-legged lope.

"Let's make it snappy. I've still got to go to the station and sign out for the day." He pushed the door almost shut, then went over to the window and stared at the traffic three floors below.

Camille sat down at the jury table and got out her yellow tablet, acting as though she had all the time in the world. "The gun," she said. "Where's the gun?"

"Locked in the evidence room, of course. Initialed, labeled and dated. You're not going to find a single problem with the chain of custody from the time the gun was removed from the defendant's hands until it goes into evidence at her trial. If that's what you're going to base your defense on, forget it. I did the drill on that one myself."

He was almost smug. From anybody else, the words would have been cocky, egotistical. From this man, though, it seemed to be no more than the confidence borne of years of careful, methodical police work. How Camille envied him that easy self-assurance. He didn't have to boast and swagger or put on a show to prove to the world how great he was. He was good at his job and believed in himself all the way to the marrow of his bones. Rock-solid, she thought. "I'll look at the chain of custody later," she replied with just enough tartness in her voice to let him know she'd be detailing his work under a microscope. "I want to know about fingerprints on the gun. Did you send it to the lab for tests?"

"Lady, this wasn't some gun we found at the side of the road. The gun was taken at the scene of the crime. The defendant dropped it into my empty plastic evidence bag with her own little hands. Why should we send it for prints?" He controlled the irritation in his voice, but his clenched fist gave him away.

"So you didn't send it for prints? That's a problem. Will you see that it goes to the lab immediately? If you'll take care of that when you go back to the station this afternoon, we might have a preliminary report by the weekend." As she scribbled on her tablet, Pike came around and read over her shoulder.

"No, ma'am, I won't send it to the lab today. I'm off duty, remember? And the prosecutor may have something to say about whether we send it for fingerprinting."

"Oh, I think Dorcas will approve. She'd have a hard time explaining to the jury why she refused such a simple request. The jury might wonder whether somebody else's prints were on that gun besides Jenny's. It might cause them to have a reasonable doubt about her guilt."

Pike's glance met hers, weighing what he observed against what he'd heard about Camille. "I guess they're wrong about you. They always said you were like a camellia, beautiful but too soft and fragile for the courtroom." He emitted a dismal laugh. "I don't know where they got that idea. I'd say you were more like Solingen steel."

"I've been working on my image." Surprised by Pike's disarming candor, the words sprang forth uncensored. Sometimes personal rapport could be as helpful as a heavy-handed bluff, maybe more so. Camille actually caught herself smiling with Pike about a subject that had caused her severe emotional anguish in the not-too-distant past. Then she became serious again. It wouldn't do for him to speculate about how truly hard she'd been working on her image. He'd think she was a pushover if he knew she actually stood in front of a mirror every day and practiced jutting her jaw. Best to change the subject and get back to business. "So you'll send the gun to the fingerprint lab?"

"Yes, I'll send it. But not today." It was clear that he had his limits and couldn't be pushed beyond them.

"That's okay. There's probably nothing there, but I'm compulsive. I want the gun checked."

He nodded. "Ballistics, too?"

"Was it fired in the holdup?"

"No. She just waved it around. That's in the report."

Camille tapped her ballpoint pen against the table, her brow furrowed in thought. "Yes, ballistics, too. Like I said, I'm compulsive."

"Yeah. Me, too."

"So I hear." They exchanged wry smiles. "I guess they couldn't be wrong about *both* of us."

There was a light rap at the door and a uniformed officer stuck in his head. "Hey, Pike, we're headed back to the station. Want to have a cup of coffee with us before you check out for the day?"

"I'll catch up with you. Need about five more minutes here."

The policeman hesitated. Apparently he'd noticed as Pike restored a stern expression to his face and distanced himself by taking a step backward from Camille. Cops are careful observers, and this one was speculating. "You're sure you don't want the guys to stick around and wait for you?"

The lines had been reestablished, Pike on one side, Camille on the other. If she was ever to get any further cooperation from him, she had to give him a way to save face in front of the other cops. "You might as well go on, Lieutenant Barrett," she said. "We aren't making much progress here, anyway. I believe it'll do my client more good if I go back to my law office and start dictating motions to file with the judge. If I get a court order, I'm sure you'll be more cooperative—whether you like it or not."

Pike mumbled something that sounded like, "We'll see," and made his departure. At the door he turned to give Camille an enigmatic nod.

She had sense enough not to say anything. Instead she gathered her notes and waited until his steps faded into the distance before she emerged from the jury room. She'd started the afternoon knowing she had something to prove to herself. As things had turned out, she was going to have to prove something to Pike Barrett. Her client's fate lay in the balance.

She'd vowed to make a fresh start with her life, Camille reminded herself, and this time be tough enough to do whatever she had to. She'd better stop by the hardware store on the way home. She was going to be eating nails for breakfast from now on.

Chapter Two

"There's a Lieutenant Barrett here to see you," said Alice Gordon, Camille's secretary, over the intercom. "He doesn't have an appointment. Were you expecting him?"

"No, but it's okay, Alice. Tell him I'll be right out." Camille pushed aside the file she'd been reviewing and reached for a tube of bright red lipstick in her desk drawer, then ran a comb through her short blond hair. Today she was wearing a black-and-white houndstooth jacket with a skinny black suede skirt. She looked good and knew it, but as she hurried to the reception area, she found herself wondering why she cared what Pike Barrett thought of her looks. A local cop, a decent enough guy... and enticing in a certain offbeat, totally masculine way. Still, he was certainly no feast to the eyes with his rumpled suit and weathered face. Besides, he was probably married with three kids and coached a soccer team on the weekends.

"Nice to see you again," she said, offering her hand as Pike unfolded himself from the too-low, too-soft sofa in the reception area and stood to greet her. He had a good handshake, firm without scrunching her fingers the way some strongman types did. Yes, a nice handshake, but not much of a smile. He was definitely the serious type. This wasn't going to be a casual visit. And he didn't seem to know how to start, so he just kept standing there shaking her hand.

Camille gave him an easy smile, hoping to relax him a little. "How about a cup of coffee?" she asked, extricating her hand and leading him toward her office in the back.

"Yeah, thanks. It's cold and drizzly outside. Something hot would taste pretty good."

She stopped off at the kitchenette. "Black?" she asked, pouring the steaming liquid into a bright red mug.

"Cream and sugar if you have it," he requested.

Camille made the additions, then poured a second cup, black, for herself. "This way," she said when he started to sit down at the small coffee table. "We'll have more privacy in my office. This coffee room is usually running over with people."

He seemed to tower over her as they walked down the hall, his shadow looming far ahead of hers. His footsteps sounded solid, belying that lankiness of his. There must be plenty of muscle on his overlong limbs.

"Nice office," he said, taking his time to look it over. Camille's office was far from the traditional leather and mahogany preferred by many lawyers. Her desk had a smoky-gray marble top, and most of the furnishings were charcoal with a few small accent pieces of red—an ashtray, a vase, a bookend. There were just enough potted plants to make the air smell fresh and clean; otherwise the office was sparsely decorated, relying for effect on the bright primary colors of modern art prints. "Thanks. I spend most of my time here, so I want it to seem like home." Rather than sitting down behind her desk, Camille deliberately chose one of the armside chairs and indicated the one beside her to Pike. She didn't know why he was here, but she could tell he wasn't exactly comfortable about it. She didn't want her desk to come between them.

The silence lengthened, interrupted only by long swallows of scalding coffee and the drumming of Pike's fingers on the arm of his chair. She could feel him studying her, and for some reason it made her feel an odd shyness. The third time his glance strayed to her legs, he caught himself and faced forward, staring at a print of red poppies on the opposite wall. Camille felt color rise in her face and wondered if her scalp had turned pink with embarrassment, the way it used to when she was a towheaded child.

When the silence became unendurable, they both spoke at once.

"Look, I'm not going to bite—"

"I wanted to thank you for getting me off the hook—"

They laughed, and the tension was eased.

"What brings you to my office today? It's not exactly one of your stop-off points for special crimes."

"The fingerprint report you wanted came in just as I went off duty, so I thought I'd run by with a copy for you to look at." Pike reached into his inside breast pocket and pulled out a typewritten document.

Camille took it from him with unabashed curiosity, not only for the contents of the report, but for why he'd done something so unusual as to deliver it himself rather than have her go to the police station or the district attorney's office to see it. It must be his way of thanking her for her parting remarks at the courthouse earlier in the week. He'd apparently noticed and appreciated her efforts to help him save face in front of the other cops.

"So the fingerprints are definitely Jenny's," she said when she'd finished reading.

"All over the place. At least eleven good prints."

"Anything else show up?"

"Nothing significant. There's one print they couldn't line up with her match-points, but it was smudged. They couldn't match it to anything else in the local files, either. That happens all the time with bad prints."

Camille sighed and put down the report. "Eleven good prints. Why didn't Jenny just sign her name to her own arrest warrant?"

"She was pretty stupid, all right. But most criminals are. The problem is that they endanger innocent people in the process. What if her victim had tried to protect himself and she'd shot him?"

"I just can't understand why she'd commit an armed robbery. She's never shown any sign of violent behavior before. All she ever did was run away. People tend to be true to type and either fight or flee. Jenny's the type that flees."

"Except if she's cornered. All crooks fight when they're cornered."

"But Jenny wasn't in a corner. She had her life straightened out, for heaven's sake. You saw that cute dress she was wearing at the courthouse, and her hair was shiny and clean. She's come a long way from that dirty-faced kid wearing clothes from a ragbag."

Pike shook his head. "I'm a cop. I worry about *what* the defendant has done. I leave the *why's* to psychiatrists and social workers."

"And lawyers. Because it's the *why* that tells a lawyer how to defend the case."

"Get the defendant off, you mean?" His jaw set in a stubborn line.

"It's my job to represent Jenny as vigorously as I can. That's the way our system works. I've sworn to protect and defend the Constitution, and that's what it requires of me. I'm not just defending some poor schmuck who got caught, I'm defending the American way of life.''

Pike nodded. "I understand how you feel. But that doesn't make her innocent.''

"*Presumed* innocent, though, until proven guilty in a court of law.''

"And that's where I come into the picture. I've got my job, just like you've got yours. That's the American way, too, isn't it?''

"Why do you have it in for Jenny?''

Pike's lips formed a thin, white line, but he didn't raise his voice. "I'm not Jenny's judge. I'm an eyewitness to her bungled attempt at armed robbery. Criminals like her are a menace to society, waving handguns around and threatening innocent people. Next time she might shoot somebody. So if I can see to it that she's locked up where she can't harm anyone, I'll do it.''

"But she's just a kid, Pike. Going to prison isn't going to make a better person out of her, it'll only make her worse. With the right kind of help, she can still be rehabilitated. You're being hard-hearted to want to throw her in jail and toss away the key.''

"And you're being softheaded to think a scared, crazy kid with a gun can't kill an innocent bystander just as dead as a hardened criminal would.''

Their gazes met, locked. Neither would yield. The silence grew until Camille could hear her own pulse pounding in her throat. The expression on Pike's face told her he felt the same angry, spewing self-righteousness that she felt. They'd struck sparks over competing principles that were buried in bedrock in their characters. Neither would ever win this argument, not while the other could draw breath. Suddenly Camille stuck out her hand. "Truce?" she said, her voice as grim as a tolling bell. "You have your job. I have mine. The system needs both of us, fully committed, in order to work. We don't have to like each other, but we're both professionals. Surely we can *respect* each other."

Pike's big, firm hand wrapped around hers and gripped hard. An electric current pulsed and sizzled with the contact. "Truce," he agreed. He let go her hand and stared at his own for a minute, as though to see whether she'd left some kind of burn mark on him. "But I never said I didn't like you."

Almost before Camille realized what had happened, Pike was on his feet and out the door.

Camille spent the next half hour pacing the floor and slapping the door facing with a manila folder. Neither activity had taken away her frustration, but she'd gotten rid of enough tension to go objectively through every word she and Pike had exchanged. Here she was with a client in big trouble and her case scheduled to be presented to the grand jury soon. There was no doubt Jenny would be indicted. So far Camille didn't have even a hint as to a possible trial strategy.

She tapped a pencil against the edge of her desk. There had to be a way to help Jenny. No client was so guilty that there wasn't some way to mount a defense. Wasn't that what her ex-husband, Marty Thorpe, had always said? In the past Camille had fought with Marty about some of his defense tactics, but she had to give him credit. Marty was a brilliant strategist, and most of the time he won.

Marty won his cases, but Camille used to lose hers. It had made for all kinds of problems between them, because not only werc they husband and wife, they were also law partners. Her losses hurt the partnership's reputation, and finally she became a luxury Marty couldn't afford. Not if he was going to join the ranks of Texas's legendary criminal lawyers. So Camille had been expendable because she just didn't measure up. She wasn't tough enough.

Marty said she tried cases with her heart, not her head. What else had he said? "Hell, Camille, with you in the courtroom, they don't even need to send in a prosecutor. You can't make yourself get down and dirty to take advantage of people. The juries love you, Camille. They love your idealism and your fighting spirit. But they vote against you anyway because they can read you like a book. They know your client is guilty. And Camille, that's ruining our business. The word is out that you're losing almost every case you touch. Don't you think it's time to admit you're not tough enough to be a criminal lawyer and go into something like probate or real-estate law?''

That had been a year ago. Marty had eased her out of their law partnership, and in almost no time afterward, he'd eased himself out of their marriage. Austin was still a small enough city that the courthouse regulars all knew one another. There'd been a lot of speculation, about the divorce as well as the partnership. There were days when Camille's neck ached from trying to hold up her head in public. Inside she'd been numb, little more than a sleepwalker. But bit by bit she'd pulled herself together, learned to hide her feelings, learned how to act tough. Things were finally beginning to come together for her again. Until this damned court-appointment came along. Two hundred and fifty dollars from Travis County, emotional bankruptcy for Camille. An open-and-shut armed robbery committed right before the eyes of Pike Barrett, head of the special crimes unit! If Fate wanted a good laugh on Camille, it couldn't have picked a better situation.

She sighed, then reached for the telephone and dialed a familiar number. "Cissy," she said to the receptionist of her good friend and rising young criminal attorney Geoff Vance, "this is Camille. Is Geoff around? I really need to talk to him."

"Sorry, Camille. He's still at the courthouse, waiting on a jury to come in."

"Oh, that's right. I'd heard the Dirkson case was going to trial this week. It's a big one for him."

"Yeah. He said if he wins it, he'll give me a bonus. We've worked a lot of overtime the last few weeks.

Have you seen the television newscasts? They've had interviews with Geoff every night. The publicity has been super. The phones are ringing off the hook.''

"That's great. Maybe this is his big break." Camille felt happy for her friend, though his perpetual success sometimes threatened her own faltering self-confidence. Geoff made everything look so easy! "If he's not too tired when he gets back from the court-house, ask him to call me, will you? I want to pick his brain about a case I'm working on. It's one of those lost causes that's right down his alley.''

Pike Barrett drove across the narrow ribbon of the Colorado River into South Austin, his windshield wipers on low. On an impulse he stopped at a grocery store. Joe Friday, his black Labrador retriever, was almost out of dog food. Besides, it was going to be a miserable November night. He might as well cook up a big pot of chili, maybe make some tacos. There might even be something decent on TV tonight for a change. He'd pick up some magazines in the grocery store, just in case he needed them. And he had some files to work on. Plenty to keep him busy and get him through the evening. If the rain let up, he'd take Joe Friday for a run. Might even do it anyway. Cold weather never bothered Joe.

He slammed the door of his pickup and made a quick trip through the grocery store, throwing in an odd assortment of masculine essentials: popcorn, razor blades, beer. After he'd scooped up his chili fixings, he headed for the toiletries section for toothpaste. He'd squeezed out the last dab at home this morning. He wheeled his cart past women's cosmetics and accidentally caught sight of himself in a mirror.

He stopped the cart and walked closer to his reflected image. Did he really look that unkempt? He smoothed down cowlicks, then eyed his wrinkled collar and ran a hand over his cheek. He realized it rasped from his day's growth of beard as well as roughened skin. He'd never been vain or considered himself a triple-threat rival to film stars like Clint Eastwood and Burt Reynolds—but in the not-too-distant past he'd certainly been able to catch the attention of a good-looking woman. How long had he been slipping bit by bit and not even noticed it? Five years? Ever since Annie had—

His mouth twisted. No use thinking about that now. He stood still a moment longer, rigid with painful memories. Then he turned the cart around and went slowly back down the aisle, tossing in something from every shelf. New hairbrushes, shampoo with built-in conditioner, after-shave, men's talcum powder, dry skin lotion. He even bought two brand-new toothbrushes. He started back to the cleaning supplies section to get some spray starch for his shirts, then changed his mind. Tomorrow was his day off. He'd go out to the mall and buy some new shirts, maybe even a couple of suits and some ties. He hadn't spent money on his wardrobe in a long time, just socked most of his paycheck into a savings account. It was time he treated himself like a human being instead of a police-procedure robot. He was only thirty-seven. If he got himself slicked up, he might not be half-bad.

Geoff Vance returned Camille's telephone call just after five o'clock that evening. He seemed elated. Another "hopeless case" had just received an acquittal. "The TV station did a nice, long interview," he said, his deep baritone voice sounding warm and happy. "Of course I was properly modest and said it was a triumph for truth, justice and the American way."

"I suppose if you ever get bored with law, you can still consider a career in drama."

"Like I always say, the courtroom is just a big indoor stage. Lawyers *are* actors, Camille. The good ones, anyway."

"Tell me how to rehearse for a case Judge Michelsohn dropped in my lap, will you? I've studied it till I'm blue in the face and I still can't come up with an angle." Camille went over all the details she had, and Geoff asked several probing questions about the evidence.

"You're court-appointed on this?" he asked finally. "Just the minimum fee, two hundred and fifty bucks? Nothing for experts or additional investigation. Jeeze, Camille, I don't think *I* could do much with this one. How can you invest time to poke around when you're not getting paid to do anything more than show up at the courthouse?''

"It doesn't matter about the money," Camille objected. "The judge appointed me to the case, and I've got to give it my best shot. Jenny isn't a bad kid, at least I don't think she is. She's entitled to a good defense."

"Yeah, but you can't put her on the witness stand with that bad attitude of hers and the chance she might fall apart in front of a jury. They'll get mad and give her a long sentence if she throws another temper tantrum like she did at the arraignment."

"Did you hear about it?"

"Yeah. Not much juicy gossip to gnaw on, so the courthouse is buzzing about your case. By the way, I heard you pushed Pike Barrett into a corner about the amount of bail. Congratulations. They said you were as smooth as silk."

Camille felt a warm inner glow. It was the first time Geoff had ever given her a compliment about her work. "Thanks, but it didn't do much good. The judge gave him a chance to qualify his testimony, and the bail was still more than Jenny could pay."

"You know, Camille, there's one possibility you might consider—" Geoff broke off, trying to think through her case. "You know the elementary rule about defending someone on an open-and-shut case. You don't let the State try *your* client. Instead turn the courtroom into a circus. *You* put on a show and divert attention from Jenny by putting *someone else* on trial. It could be the holdup victim, or maybe an eyewitness, a cop, even the prosecutor. What about Pike Barrett? He's tough, but he's human. He's bound to have a fatal flaw in his history somewhere.''

Camille didn't like what she was hearing. "What do you mean?''

"Make him look like a fool to the jury. Discredit his testimony. Find something about him to make it look like he has a reason for picking on your client. Maybe he's got a thing about cute young blondes. Maybe chicks with guns turn him on. Who knows? But find his weak spot and hammer it.''

"Oh, Geoff, I couldn't do that—''

There was a moment's silence. Then Geoff said kindly, "No, Camille, I don't believe you could. It isn't your style, is it? Forget I even mentioned it. You're not lean-and-mean enough for that kind of tactic.''

Camille let out a deep, shuddering breath. So be it. She'd find another way. She wasn't going to use a tactic that would destroy a decent human being like Pike Barrett in the process of winning her case. "Well, Geoff, now you know where they got that expression for the first women who went to law school. I'm just another petticoat lawyer.''

There was a startled laugh, quickly repressed. "Never mind, Camille. In the old days it was a derogatory term coined by male lawyers who didn't want to admit women were as tough and capable as they were. In your case, petticoat lawyer means a classy female who treats everybody with respect. Take it as a compliment.'' Then, as though he realized her pain, he added more gently, ''Sorry I couldn't help, sweetie. But you'll come up with something that'll work, I'm sure of it. See you around the courthouse, okay? And don't forget to watch me on the ten o'clock news.''

Pike Barrett unloaded his groceries and looked around his small South Austin duplex as though he hadn't seen it in months. Why hadn't he ever noticed that this duplex was like a motel, all drab earthtones and nothing personal about the furnishings? Things were neat enough, with dishes clean in the dishwasher and the bed made. He wandered through the house, taking off his suit and hanging it in the closet, then changing into jogging clothes. He went to the back door and whistled for Joe Friday, who came bounding to meet him. Pike squatted on the floor and wrapped the wet Lab in a towel, roughhousing until they were both damp with rain and sweat. Joe pulled loose and put his paws on Pike's shoulders, then tried to lick his face.

''None of your messy kisses,'' Pike objected, twisting away from the dog's wet tongue. For a moment he felt like a little boy again, carried back to childhood by the animal's smell and touch. An unexpected lump formed in Pike's throat, and moisture filled his eyes before he could blink it away. ''It's a good thing I've got you to keep me company.'' Pike buried his head against Joe's shoulder and gave him a love-pat on the flank. "What do you say, Joe? Want to go for a run? Check out the neighborhood and see if any new dogs have moved in? Eat your dog food while I put my chili on the stove to simmer, and then we'll see if we can't run off some of our excess energy."

A thirty-minute run should've vented Pike's pent-up restlessness, but it didn't. Neither did cooking a meal, cleaning up the dishes and straightening everything in the house. He even scoured the bathroom, took a shower, and tried out his new after-shave. Afterward, sprawled on the sofa in his terry-cloth robe, he aimlessly flipped channels with the remote control and thumbed through a sports magazine. But nothing seemed to capture his attention.

He pulled the table lamp closer and forced himself to read a story about the erratic football season of the Dallas Cowboys. Coach Tom Landry must be having the last laugh about getting fired. Pike looked at his watch. It was only ten o'clock. This had to be one of the longest days of his life. It seemed as though at least three weeks must have passed since this afternoon when he'd stopped by Camille Clark's law office. And gotten in an argument with her. How on earth had it happened? They'd been just talking, and all at once, sparks were flying. He must've stomped on her toes pretty good, because she was one mad motor scooter. Those big, brown eyes of hers were flashing fire. About the *Constitution*, for crying out loud! It was a little hard on a guy's ego to think a woman could get herself so worked up and passionate about a two-hundred-year-old piece of paper when there was a flesh-and-blood male smack-dab in front of her nose.

It was a cute nose, too, tilted a little at the end. In fact, the whole package was pretty spectacular: great legs, tight little body, luscious red lips . . .

Pike stomped into the kitchen barefooted and got a cold beer from the refrigerator. You know what's the matter with you, wise guy? he asked himself, flipping the top on the beer with a beady-eyed scowl. You've been walking around in a fog for months, and somebody finally told you the sun's come out. Camille Clark has gotten under your skin and given you a sunburn, and you don't know what to do about it. You're completely out of practice. You don't even know how to ask a woman for a date anymore. She's a tiny little thing, not more than five-six to your six-three, but you're scared to death of her.

He slammed the refrigerator door and padded back into the living room with his beer. For a long time he stared at the TV screen without seeing the program that was on. Then without really knowing why he was doing something so impulsive and out of character, he reached for the telephone directory and looked to see whether there was a residential listing for Camille. There was. He picked up the telephone and dialed her number.

"Why, hello, Pike." Camille was flustered. She'd been brooding about him all evening, ever since she'd had her ill-fated conversation with Geoff. Pike's telephone call made her feel guilty, as though somehow he must've found out about Geoff's suggested scheme to discredit his testimony.

"I hope I haven't called too late."

"No. I was just watching the news." She didn't bother to mention that she'd been watching Geoff's television interview. It had been an incredible performance. Geoff looked handsome and sincere, saying all the right things about democracy and the jury system. Geoff was definitely headed for the big time. Maybe even politics, the way he could charm a camera. And he was a good friend. Even though he was disappointed that Camille wouldn't take his advice, he didn't criticize her. Instead he complimented her. Didn't matter, though. She knew what he really thought. That she didn't have what it took to be a criminal lawyer. What if he was right? That was the question that haunted her. Camille realized she wasn't paying attention to what Pike was saying and tried to shake off her doubts and depression.

"Look," Pike said, his voice strained and the words sounding a little awkward. "I want to apologize about the blowup this afternoon. I don't know what got into me. I never lose my temper that way."

"Don't apologize, really," she said. "I was just as angry as you were." She thought back over their conversation and the ensuing argument. "That's not to say that I agree with everything you said, because I don't. But it's a difference of philosophies, and there's no need to get nasty about it."

"So you really meant it when you offered a truce?"

"Sure. Didn't you?"

"Well, yeah."

There was another of those lengthy silences that she'd come to expect from Pike. She had no doubt that when physical action was required, he'd be hard to beat—but he certainly had difficulty with words. She tried to wait while he worked his way to whatever it was he wanted to say to her, but she was so depressed about everything that had happened that the extended silence wore her down. "It was very nice of you to phone," she said, ready to terminate the call.

"Yeah, well, my grandma said never let the sun go down on your anger. I wanted to try to set things right before I went to bed tonight." He cleared his throat. "I'm going to be off duty tomorrow, but I'll be checking in with the station. If the ballistics report comes in on Jenny's gun, I'll see that you get a copy."

"Thanks. That'll help." This offer, seemingly genuine, was totally out of character for Pike. At least based on his reputation and what she'd seen for herself. "You said you were compulsive. Does that mean you can't even take a day off without police work following you around?"

"Sometimes I think a cop is never really off duty."

"Then I guess the taxpayers get their money's worth out of you. They pay you for eight hours and you work around the clock. Don't you ever take time out for fun?"

"Sometimes." He cleared his throat again. "In fact, I was thinking about taking in a barbecue and band tomorrow night. Asleep at the Wheel is playing at the Broken Spoke."

It figured that he'd be a country music fan.

"I don't suppose you can dance the Cotton-Eyed Joe, can you?"

"Come on. I'm a Texan, aren't I?" For goodness' sake. In his own boyish, endearing way, Pike was asking her for a date. But what about that wife and kids and soccer team she'd imagined him having? He certainly didn't strike her as a typical predatory bachelor. Decent, thoughtful, soft-spoken—he was at least semidomesticated. "Are you asking me to go out with you tomorrow night?"

"Well, yeah, didn't I say so?"

"Well, yeah, I think you did." Camille mimicked his phrasing in a teasing way that made him laugh and gave her a little time to think. Her spirits were lower tonight than they'd been in months. She'd come face-to-face with the fact that she might not be cut out to be a criminal lawyer, and it was the only career she'd ever considered. It meant everything to her. She'd walked the floors and wrung her hands and brooded the entire evening. She couldn't go through another night like this one. She didn't know what it would be like to dance the Cotton-Eyed Joe with Pike Barrett, but even if he stomped all over her feet, it would be better than another night spent stomping her own ego into smithereens. "I'll make a deal with you," she said. "I already have plans for dinner, but I'll meet you at the Broken Spoke in time for the band. Will nine o'clock be okay?"

There was no change in the tone of his voice. If he was disappointed, he didn't let it show. "Nine o'clock is fine. I'll meet you at the front."

"Just one thing," Camille said. "Remember that we can't talk about Jenny's case. You're a witness for the State, and I can't discuss the case with you unless the prosecutor is present or gives her permission. Okay?"

"Sure," he answered. "I promise you, Jenny's case has nothing to do with this telephone call. It's strictly personal."

It was too bad he couldn't see Camille's mischievous grin. "In that case, then," she said, "I'll be the one in tight jeans."

Chapter Three

Pike Barrett leaned against the doorjamb in the entryway to the Broken Spoke, Austin's legendary country-and-western dance hall, and listened for approaching footsteps. He checked his watch again. Nine o'clock sharp. He'd been standing here since eight-thirty waiting for Camille to arrive, and with every passing minute he'd become more convinced she was going to stand him up.

He looked around the club. Legendary it might be, but part of its reputation was based on twenty-five years without any changes—including cosmetic repairs. The parking lot was full of potholes, the dining tables were antiquated picnic leftovers, the crowd eclectic but not many professionals among them.

What had made him suggest a place like this to a classy and sophisticated woman like Camille Clark, who would be much more at home in a country club setting? Except that Pike Barrett didn't belong to a country club. Never had and never would. That wasn't his life-style. Which made it even more obvious that he and Camille weren't in the same league, so why in the name of heaven had he made a fool of himself by asking her for a date?

He tightened his fist in annoyance at his own stupidity. He'd been doing just fine in his self-imposed hermitage. Five years of feeling nothing, and feeling nothing had become a pleasure indeed. So much better than the terrible, never-ending, gut-wrenching pain he'd felt when he'd lost Annie, his sweet wife, five years ago.

Don't think about that now, Barrett. The past is finished. Let it go. If you think about it, all that pain is going to come back, and you'll never beat it down again.

Work, hard work, nothing but work, had slowly wrapped its coils around him and day by day had brought him a little peace, a little surcease from his pain. For five years he'd been a caterpillar, gradually spinning a cocoon around himself to protect himself from the outside world. How stupid he'd been to think of leaving his safe haven where he was insulated from all feeling! How could he have let down his guard so Camille Clark could pierce his protecting armor?

Now here he was, eyeing his watch and feeling his ego being demolished because he'd set his sights on the wrong woman. No way he could've made a worse choice for his own laid-back, sober style than by picking a bright, vivacious personality. Now Camille would crush his pride under her heel by standing him up. It was nine-fifteen. She wasn't coming. He might as well go home and try to pretend it didn't matter, that it never happened. But how was he going to face her the next time he ran into her at the courthouse? Look the other way? Confront her? Make a joke about it? Pike gripped the doorjamb with one clenched hand. He wanted to pound the wall, but this was a public place and the hostess was watching him. If she asked him once more if he wanted to use the phone to check on his party, he knew he'd lose it.

He felt choked with anger—anger at Camille, anger at the hostess, anger at himself, anger at the world. He didn't like these relentless feelings that made him lose some of his stern self-control. He didn't like these feelings that made him vulnerable to someone he hardly knew. Most of all, he didn't like these feelings that stripped his defenses and left him with so much pain. He'd been a fool, but it wouldn't happen again. He swallowed hard against the lump in his throat and forced his mind to detach itself, and him along with it, from this moment of misery. Slowly his anger died, slowly he brought his emotions under control. His face paled and stiffened in a nondescript smile. It was time to go home, back to his old life with no expectations, no joy, no grief. He'd made a mistake, but it had only cost him an hour. He nodded to the hostess and stepped from the doorway.

"Sorry I'm late," Camille said, hurrying through the entry to the Broken Spoke and almost bumping into Pike. "My planning meeting ran overtime."

She didn't like feeling so rushed and thrown together. She was still tying the bright sash at the waist of her blue denim skirt as she made her hasty apology. It was nine twenty-five. Her dinner meeting with an Austin civic group had run late, and she'd had to run by her house to change clothes afterward.

"You made it after all," Pike said, his lips twisting into something that looked like a cross between a scowl and a grin. The angry relief in his expression told her he'd wondered whether she was going to show up.

She tried to make up for her tardiness by giving him a warm smile. "The committee couldn't decide whether to use our extra funds for a scholarship or a lecture series. They haggled over it for an hour. Isn't that typical of Austin?"

He must've believed her apology, because now his lips formed the merest hint of a smile, gone before it ever reached his dark eyes. "So while you were dying of boredom in a committee free-for-all, I had the pleasure of checking out all the good-looking blondes in tight britches trying to figure out which one was you." He gave her full, calf-length skirt an appraising glance. "Thought you said you'd be wearing jeans?"

"Oh, I changed my mind. This skirt is better for dancing. It has a ruffled pettitcoat that drives men wild when I shake my foot during the Cotton-Eyed Joe. Besides, these are my best cowboy boots. You wouldn't want me to hide them under a pair of jeans, would you?"

Their bantering stopped as Pike took her hand and made a path for them through a crowd of enthusiastic spectators and dancers. It was welcome-home night for Asleep at the Wheel, a local band that had made good and was now on the national charts. Pike located an empty table at the far edge of the dance floor and held a chair for Camille to be seated. A cruising waitress appeared almost instantaneously to take their drink orders.

"How about some beer and nachos?" the waitress asked.

"Sounds great to me," Pike said. "How about you, Camille?"

"I think I'll stick with diet cola."

The waitress nodded and left in a flurry, taking orders from other tables on her way back to the kitchen. Pike still seemed a little tense, and Camille wondered what was wrong. Maybe he'd changed his mind and wished he hadn't made a date with her. After all, they scarcely knew each other, and all their previous contacts had put them on opposite sides of the fence. He probably regretted having to spend an evening with someone where he'd have to be on guard every moment.

Camille was beginning to feel the same way herself. What had come over her last night, making her agree to this date? She'd felt so lonely and depressed that she'd thought anything would be better than spending another evening alone. She'd been mistaken. It would be much harder to spend an evening with an observant cop. Maybe she'd wait for a decent interval, then make her excuses and escape.

She lifted her head and gave Pike her first real scrutiny. He'd gotten his hair cut, but it was dark and thick and still long enough at the nape to wave against his collar with a casual sexiness. His plaid shirt— which looked crisp and new—eased and strained with the slightest motion of his shoulders. He projected some kind of animal magnetism that made Camille feel a little confused, a little less certain that she'd leave at the first opportune moment.

Pike settled his long frame into his chair and gave her a searching look. "I imagine you're the type who drinks French wine and eats fancy baked cheese. I should've thought of that before I asked you to come to a down-home place like this. A beer joint's not your style."

Camille tried to set him at ease. "Now, Pike, would I own a pair of cowboy boots and have a square-dance skirt in my closet if I didn't enjoy a country-and-western club?" She leaned forward and put her hand on Pike's forearm. "Don't jump to conclusions and sell me short. I've been to the Broken Spoke before. I like doing a little kicker dancing."

His scowl remained a moment longer, and he ran his palm across his furrowed brow. "I'm more out of practice than I realized," he muttered.

"At what?"

He gave her an abashed glance. "At dating. It's like being an awkward teenager all over again."

Pike seemed like the kind of guy to have a houseful of kids and a dog—the domesticated type. She'd even envisioned him coaching a soccer team. Probably he was recently divorced, as she was. She wouldn't ask him any curious questions, though. He might not want to talk about it. Maybe it would help him to know other people experienced the same kind of ineptness when they had to pick up the pieces of their lives and start over.

"Me, too," she said, a little wistfully. "The first few times I went out after my divorce, I was so nervous I almost decided to give up on myself. I worried that I talked too fast or wore the wrong clothes or was a complete bore." She betrayed herself with a laugh that sounded tinny and strained in her own ears. "Guess I'm not over it yet," she admitted. "Am I talking too much?"

"Surely *I* don't make you nervous?" Pike lowered his chair to the floor with a surprised plop. "A sophisticated chick like you with all the guys watching every move you make?"

Camille's eyes clouded with pain. "Having everybody watch is what's so bad about it. Everybody at the courthouse is waiting to see if I'll make one false move. They'd love to know what happened between Marty and me and all the lurid details of the divorce.''

Pike reached for her hand and held it, as though the gentle brush of his thumb could wipe away her hurt. "That bad, huh?" he said, not seeming to expect a response.

She shrugged her shoulders. "It hurt. But I guess I'll live." Her hand turned palm up inside his, and for a moment she gripped hard. "The worst part is having your private anguish exposed in public. I have to psych myself up every time I go to the courthouse." She felt her eyes grow moist. What a long time it had been since a man had simply held her hand and shared her emotional suffering. Their eyes met, and something sparked between them. Camille's stomach somersaulted, her pulse raced. "Now I know I'm talking too much," she said breathlessly. "Let's get out on the dance floor and try our luck at the Texas two-step."

There was something responsive in Pike's expression, and it made Camille even more adventuresome. All at once she knew she wanted to feel his arms around her. He'd make her feel safe. No, she realized, glancing into his dark eyes. He made her feel dangerous. And she liked the feeling. Her throat was too constricted to speak, so she reached for his hand. Pike followed her onto the dance floor.

Camille's head came to just the right point at Pike's shoulder that he could curl her against its protective hollow and settle his chin against her silky, fragrant hair. The band had started with a slow number, giving time for the dancers to warm up and giving time for Pike's body to settle in and adjust to the contours of Camille's. His hand moved up her back, and she leaned against him, her breasts soft against his chest. Pike closed his eyes and inhaled slowly, trying on some primitive level to draw her femininity into himself. The music permitted a kind of instant intimacy normally forbidden to near strangers, and though his body leaned close, seeking hers, Pike's mind went through a series of warnings to himself to keep it cool. Their dance became an awkward two-step—advance physically, retreat emotionally, let yourself go, pull back.

As though she sensed his hesitation, Camille lifted her head from his shoulder, her eyes questioning.

"Sorry," he said. "Haven't been dancing in quite a while. Guess I've forgotten how." The band shifted into a livelier number, and Pike swung Camille toward the center of the dance floor and into a crush of other couples that made talking impossible. There were so many dancers and they were all moving so fast that it was all he could do to keep from stomping on someone's feet. But by the time the number ended, he and Camille were dancing in perfect rhythm. Pike realized he was a much better dancer when he kept his mind on the motions of his own feet rather than on the fluid movement of the female body he held in his arms.

The band moved immediately into the Cotton-Eyed Joe. Camille's brown eyes sparkled with fun as she twirled her skirts and kicked and shouted with the crowd until the set ended, then fell laughing against Pike's chest.

Some unbidden impulse seized him, and he dropped an undetectable kiss against her silky crown. "You're good at this," he said. "I wouldn't have brought you here if I'd known you were going to show me up and be the belle of the ball."

"When it comes to the Cotton-Eyed Joe, you just have to let yourself go. It's no dance for the cautious of spirit."

"Cautious? Me?" Pike blocked a path for them through the crowd, and they returned to their table, now furnished with cold nachos and warm beer. He signaled for their waitress while he ruminated on Camille's comment. Every day of his life he faced danger and possible death in the line of duty. He didn't think of himself as a gung-ho warrior—but he'd never considered himself cautious, either. Being with Camille was making him probe all kinds of unexamined assumptions about his character. He wasn't sure he liked the process. In fact, he decided he didn't like it. It made him too uncomfortable. He wasn't the type for introspection and navel contemplation. He was made for action. "Why do you call me *cautious*?"

Camille's smile disappeared and her expression became serious. "Something about the way you watch everything that's going on in the room." She toyed with one of the nachos, pushing aside the cold Monterey Jack cheese and some jalapeño peppers. "Something about the way you hold yourself back, even when you swing me out into the crowd." Her eyes crinkled for a moment. "But mostly it was the way I could almost feel you counting time to the music. One-two-three-*kick*. You dance a very tidy, orderly version of the Cotton-Eyed Joe."

Pike leaned across the table and reached for Camille's hand. She popped a cold nacho into her mouth. "Live dangerously," she said with a playful smile. "Eat cold nachos. Drink warm beer. Get out of your rut."

She fed him a dollop of stringy cheese on a soggy corn chip. Pike chewed. The jalapeño peppers brought fire to his throat and tears to his eyes. He reached for his glass of warm beer and quaffed half of it. "Now am I loose enough to suit you?"

"I don't know. How loose can you get?"

Pike eyed Camille warily. What was she up to? In their previous encounters she'd been a cool, distant professional. He hadn't seen this sporting, bantering side of her before. If he'd been intimidated a little earlier by her social status, he was completely buffaloed by this new dimension. The ground was shifting too fast for him. She was right. He was a cautious person after all. And she was scaring the hell out of him.

He let go of her hand and stared into her eyes, scrutinizing what he found there. It was a strange combination of laughter, understanding and desire. Pike swallowed hard and looked around for the waitress. He was in over his head and going deeper. If the waitress didn't arrive immediately to rescue him, he was a goner for sure.

"Here you are," the waitress said, substituting a plate of hot nachos for the old ones. "I wouldn't have turned in your order a while ago if I'd known you were going onto the dance floor." She quickly rearranged the table and whisked away glasses, making change at the same time. "No more dancing till you finish your order," she scolded in a bossy way that was not only acceptable to Pike in his current mental state, but actually welcome. *No more dancing.* Not for now, not till he got his emotions back under control. On the dance floor his feelings were no secret. He wasn't ready for Camille to get to know him any better than she already did. He didn't like the idea that she could read him like a nursery rhyme. It was time to turn the tables and put the spotlight on her for a while.

He asked the question he'd wondered about the most. "What made you decide to go into criminal law? It seems like a funny choice for someone like you." He was surprised when her body tensed and her face became impassive.

"People say that all the time. Like I'm all wrong to be a criminal lawyer. But it's all I've ever wanted to do." She sat upright and pushed her hair back from her face, taking a deep breath. "Not everybody who gets charged with a crime is guilty, and even the ones who are guilty are entitled to be defended in court. That's the way our American system of justice operates. There are lots of different roles—yours, the prosecuting attorney, the judge, the bailiff and court reporter, even. But the role I want to play is the defense attorney. That's where I want to make my contribution. I want to make a difference, to protect the innocent where I can and see that the guilty get a fair trial and some kind of rehabilitation. If I can't make it as a criminal lawyer, I don't think I'll be able to live with the sense of failure. It was bad enough to have my marriage go sour, but I can't lose my career, too. It's too important to me.''

Her voice had become very low, her lips pinched tight with earnestness. There was a knot of fear she couldn't hide, and Pike saw it. It perplexed him. She seemed to care more about being able to continue her career than she did about the breakup of her marriage. There had been plenty of gossip around town, and he'd heard some of it. Her ex-husband was a hotshot full of ego and ambition, and Marty Thorpe had been the kind of jerk to place all the blame for their divorce on Camille. Though scarcely anyone believed him, except maybe Camille herself. Everyone had been curious and watched the changes in her over the past year, but the general consensus seemed to be that the changes were only superficial and that underneath, Camille was her same old self—warm, witty and determined.

Pike had never been involved with one of Camille's cases before, but he'd known her by sight and reputation the same way she'd known him. What he didn't know was what drove her. Why did she try so hard with the most hopeless cases? She took on cases that lawyers with a better sense of self-preservation would know to avoid, or resolve quickly in the district attorney's office because they were unwinnable. But not Camille. She'd fight it out in the courtroom and in the newspapers no matter how desperate the situation.

Jenny Mayner was a case in point. Open-and-shut, no way to fight, no hope to win—but nonetheless Camille was ordering fingerprint studies and ballistics checks as though she could mount a defense that would somehow get Jenny off.

"You aren't a failure, Camille," Pike said in a gentle voice. "Losing cases doesn't make you a failure. Getting a divorce doesn't make you a failure, either."

"Thanks. Even if I know better, it helps to have someone say it's okay. I can't change what's already happened, but I can try to do better the next time around." Her bright lips formed a smile. "Finish your beer so we can dance without getting the waitress in an uproar. The band is warming up for the next set, and we're both going to throw caution to the wind and get out there and wiggle." She took a last bite of nacho and downed it with cola. "On the dance floor, we can both be winners."

Winners, hell, Pike thought, three dances later. Three *slow* dances later, with Camille wrapped in his arms, her body snuggled against him, her hair feathery against his cheek. The rising heat of desire made him edgy, restless. He'd been alone too long, suppressed his passions with bone-numbing work, and was caught off guard by an unexpected attraction toward the wrong woman. Wrong for him, anyway. She opened up nooks and crannies in his memory that were better left forgotten.

As they danced, he tried to distract his physical responses to Camille by reflecting on their conversation at the table. She said she'd been hurt by her divorce, but nothing about why it had happened. Pike had always thought it took two to make a marriage and two to make a divorce. Would he and Annie have become another divorce statistic if their marriage had lasted, if she hadn't gotten killed? *Don't think about Annie's death; you can't handle the pain.* They'd had so little time together. They'd never gotten past that hot rush of the honeymoon.

And after Annie's death, Pike had retreated, unwilling to risk that kind of passion and expose himself to such grief and loss ever again. Now, when he was least expecting it, Camille—this blonde who sometimes had a chip on her shoulder, who was as unlike Annie as a woman could be—had sneaked up on his blind side and stirred feelings that he thought were dead. She aroused him, all right, but every curve of her body, every flash of her eyes told his heart to be careful.

Pike was, as he'd already discovered this evening, a cautious man. Not the kind to ignore danger signs. So even though he wanted to pull Camille close into his arms and kiss her, he was afraid of what might happen if he unleashed the depths of his long-denied physical passion.

As the last number came to a close, Pike drew away from Camille and stuffed into his pockets the hands that had taken such pleasure in holding her body against him. "Ready for something cool to drink?" he asked, and steered her toward the table. No sense giving her a chance to object. It was time to cut the evening short before they both waded into quicksand that would suck them under before they knew what was happening.

Camille let herself be led back to the table without making a protest. Clearly something had suddenly gone wrong. One minute they were dancing and having fun, the next minute Pike was moving away from her with all the speed of a flying bullet. What was wrong with her, that she had this effect on men? She'd thought it was pleasant to glide around the dance floor in Pike's arms, but it certainly hadn't affected him the same way. She racked her brain for the answer.

Probably it was because she'd let down her guard and let him get to know her as a person rather than as a professional playing a specific role. She'd been pretty hard-boiled in their previous contacts, and that was what he was expecting from her. There it was again. *Tough.* Pike was a tough cop, and he liked people as tough as he was. He wasn't interested in a woman who got all weepy-eyed about the trauma and scars from her divorce. He wasn't interested in a woman who waxed emotional about her commitment to her profession. He wasn't interested in a woman who yielded herself to his arms on the dance floor.

Heaven forbid that he ever find out she was a brass-plated marshmallow. Tough guys had no use for people who were mush on the inside. Like Camille. Pike's rejection ignited the fuse to her inner insecurity, but she was a good enough actress to hide her misery from him. Camille got hold of herself and tilted her chin to its jutting angle, squared her shoulders until they seemed broad enough to include football shoulder-pads. This man was *never* going to find out how vulnerable she was inside. And especially not how vulnerable he made her feel. They could torture her by hammering toothpicks through her fingernails but she wouldn't confess the truth.

She ordered a very expensive label of Scotch, neat, and drank it with all the toughness she could muster. When her knees went weak and her throat began to burn, she decided it was time to call it a night. She and Pike obviously had nothing in common and nothing to talk about. Next time she'd stay home and read a good book. It was less depressing than a fiasco like this.

She gave Pike a glittering smile. "I didn't realize it had gotten so late," she said. "I have a client coming into the office early in the morning. I really must be going."

"Tomorrow's Saturday."

"Yes, I know. My office is open on Saturday mornings."

"Oh. Well, I have to work, too. Guess it's time to call it a night."

"There's no need for you to leave now. I'll be on my way, but why don't you stay and enjoy the band? They'll be back after intermission."

Pike shook his head. "I'll see you to your car."

"That's not necessary, really." At the moment, Camille wanted to escape his presence and the necessity to continue this facade that unfortunately seemed to be coming across more as brittle than tough. She shouldn't have drunk the Scotch so fast. It was hampering her acting ability.

Pike rose and came around to help Camille with her chair. His lips were set in a grim line. He seemed to be as eager as Camille to end this dreadful evening. He hesitated for a moment, then awkwardly wrapped her bandanna-lined denim shawl around her shoulders. "Will this be warm enough for you? It's going to be cooler now than it was when we came in tonight."

"I'll be fine. Haven't you heard, I'm made of ice and sleep in the deep-freeze to keep warm?" Camille had heard some of the gossip about her, especially the juicy comments like this one.

Pike shot her an irritated look but didn't respond. His fingers tightened, or seemed to, on her shoulders as he tried to arrange the folds of fabric. "Let's get out of here," he muttered, then added something that sounded like, "This has been quite an evening."

It was easy to make their way to the exit, now that the dancing had temporarily stopped. Traffic flowed past them on South Lamar Street, headlights dancing and casting intermittent shadows against the building. The November night was cool but not unpleasant, and the fresh air seemed to carry their frustration and disappointment away with a gentle sigh. The usual cloud cover had disappeared, leaving the stars brilliant against the midnight sky. Camille felt Pike's arm come around her as they made their way across the potholes in the parking lot.

"Watch your step," he said. "The lighting out here isn't all that great. Where's your car?"

"Over there," she answered, indicating a new, pearl-white Audi that glimmered in the moonlight. "Where's yours?"

Pike pointed to an old, but well-kept, pickup truck parked well away from Camille's car.

"You're in the other direction," she protested. "There's no need to see me to my car. It's perfectly safe."

"My grandma taught me better manners than that," Pike said. His arm tightened a little, and Camille thought if she turned around, she'd probably catch him frowning at her. Tough guys protect a lady's

honor, she thought. It was part of Pike's code. He was
born in the wrong century. He should've been one of
King Arthur's knights.

They got to Camille's car, and she dug in her purse
for her keys. The hush of the night closed in, and she
turned to tell Pike good-night. There was something
unexpected in his expression, a sort of tender longing
that he couldn't erase quickly enough to keep her from
seeing. She stood there, hand half-outstretched, while
their glances met and held. The silence lengthened,
and with it the tension. There wasn't even the sound
of their breathing, almost as though their lungs were
sustained by some kind of mystic vapor. The pulse
throbbed in Camille's throat, roared in her temples,
and she thought in another second she would either
fall in a swoon like some ladyfaire from old, or throw
herself into Pike's arms.

Abruptly Pike reached out and brushed Camille's
lips with his finger. Then he took the car keys from her
and unlocked the door. Almost in a trance, she started
the ignition and pulled the car to the curb to enter the
line of traffic. She glanced back over her shoulder.
Pike was standing in exactly the same place, the same
position. He lifted his hand in a gesture that was more
like a salute than a wave, then continued to watch as
she drove away. Camille touched her fingers to her
lips, mystified to find that they tingled as though Pike
had actually kissed her.

Chapter Four

Here's the correspondence for you to sign," said Alice Gordon as she stepped into the office, breaking Camille's train of thought. "My goodness, your mind seems to be a million miles away."

"I'm concentrating on one of my cases. You remember, the new one with Jenny Mayner? I'm still floundering with it."

"Do you want me to prepare the regular set of motions for her case? I meant to ask you about it on Monday, but we were so busy with docket call I forgot all about it." Alice was an efficient secretary with plenty of initiative who coincidentally was old enough to be Camille's mother. When Camille and Marty broke up their law partnership, Marty kept the old office with all the furnishings and law library, and Camille took Alice with her to a new office. Camille had said many times that she'd gotten far and away the best part of that bargain. Alice invested considerable maternal energy into overseeing Camille's needs and was absolutely indispensable to Camille's practice.

"I'll think about what I need for Jenny's case," Camille answered. "I may go over to the jail and talk to her before we start a flurry of paperwork." She put the stack of correspondence in the middle of her desk and quickly scanned the contents of each page before scrawling her characteristic signature with only the two capital *C*'s legible. "Is my handwriting getting worse?" she asked, peering at one signature as she waited for the ink to dry.

"How could it get any worse? Nobody but you and I can read it now, and sometimes I wonder about you." There was a twinkle in Alice's eye, but though she might dote on Camille, she certainly didn't condone any known or suspected weaknesses.

"I must be doing better," Camille said in a droll voice. "This is the first time all week you've chastised me."

"This is the first time we've had the slightest opportunity to talk about anything. My goodness, this office has been a zoo all week long."

"It's always like that after docket call. The judge sets the cases for trial and everybody goes crazy. The district attorney's office wants to make deals, the defendants suddenly decide they can't stand the thought of facing a jury, the lawyers behind you on the docket go nuts because if your case settles that means they're up for trial. That's what makes it exciting, Alice. You know you love it."

"Yes, of course. I love it. The phones ringing off the hook, the clients screaming hysterically, their families pacing the floor in front of my desk." She took the last signed letter from Camille's hand. "And policemen coming in person to deliver flowers."

Camille whirled in her chair to face Alice. "Policemen?"

"Well, singular. Policeman. I should've been more precise." Alice's dark eyes sparkled with mischief. "It was that nice young man who dropped by the office last week. He said not to disturb you. He stuck the flowers in my hand and hurried out the door as fast as those long legs of his would carry him."

Camille was already half out of her chair. "Where are they?" She hurried down the hallway ahead of Alice and discovered a delicate bud vase on the reception desk. It contained a single yellow rose accented with dark green leaves and sprigs of fern. Camille ripped open the card and read, "Dancing at the Broken Spoke will never be the same again. Pike."

Alice unabashedly read the card over Camille's shoulder. "Well, well. What does this mean?"

"I have no idea. Pike Barrett is the most perplexing man I've ever met." Camille read the card again, then focused her attention on the yellow rose. "He sends out such mixed signals. He could hardly wait to make his escape Friday night at the Broken Spoke. Now he sends me one yellow rose. If he'd sent a bouquet of red roses, I'd know what he meant. If he disappeared into thin air and I never heard from him again, I'd know what that meant. But what's the significance of one yellow rose, can you tell me that?''

She plopped down on the sofa in dismay. She'd tried to put last Friday evening out of her mind, but every now and then the memory of Pike's finger brushing her lip as they said good-night had come back to her, stirring her senses. She'd found herself wondering what Pike was thinking, or if he thought at all about that evening. Well, obviously he did. The rose was proof of that. But why deliver it in person, then leave without seeing her? Why hadn't he simply had the florist deliver it?

"I suspect he didn't want anyone to know he was sending flowers to you, not even the florist. Or maybe he wanted to be able to change his mind right up to the last minute.'' Alice was speculating aloud, apparently entertaining the same questions that Camille did. "And he wasn't sure how you'd react, so he left them with an anonymous secretary. The reason for sending a yellow rose? Maybe because it's not obvious, like red roses would be. Or he's not sure what he wants from the relationship himself?''

Alice leaned forward and touched the vase. "This isn't the kind of glass vase florists use,'' she said. "It's crystal. He bought it somewhere and took it with him to the florist. Someplace expensive, I'd say. It's very nice." She lifted the vase in Camille's hands and peeked underneath where the maker's label was glued. "Told you."

"Scotland Yard could use a woman with your investigative talents." Camille placed the vase on the coffee table in front of her and stared at it. It had been a long time since a man's behavior had been so intriguing to her.

But right now, she had to remember that Pike Barrett was a cop. She was still stumped on Jenny Mayner's case, and Pike was going to be the State's main witness. Why was he so determined to see Jenny go to prison? Was it the blood lust of a Dirty Harry mentality? Camille didn't think so. But there must be something that made him so dogged and relentless in his pursuit of criminal defendants. What had Geoff Vance said? "He's bound to have a fatal flaw in his history somewhere...maybe he's got a thing for cute young blondes...maybe chicks with guns turn him on...find his weak spot and hammer it."

Camille looked at the velvety petals of the rose blossom, inhaled its delicate fragrance. Things weren't adding up. "You've got good instincts about people," she said to Alice. "What's your reaction to Pike Barrett?"

Alice thought for a moment. "Hmmmm. He comes across as a nice young man. He's very tall, big-boned, and his size could be intimidating but somehow it's not. As though he makes an effort to be unassuming. He's quiet, doesn't say much, watches everything. I don't believe his eyes miss a thing. And you can tell he's alert, that he's ready to spring if something goes wrong. But mostly you think nothing will go wrong simply because he's there to stop trouble before it starts. I guess that's it, really."

"Is that it?" Even though Alice had affirmed many of Camille's own impressions, Camille was somehow a little disappointed that there hadn't been more. She wasn't even sure herself what she'd hoped Alice would say. But summed up that way, Pike didn't sound very interesting.

A dimple quirked at the corner of Alice's lip. "That's *my* reaction, dear, to the way he's appeared to me. Now, if I were *you*, and I had this lovely gift, I'd have a good deal more to say. That he's got good taste and an appreciation for lovely things. That he's not ostentatious, prefers things that are simple. That he knows how to create an aura of mystery and surprise. And that he was quite nice-looking before, but now that he's bought himself a new suit and spiffed himself up, he's absolutely devastating." She smiled broadly. "Will that do?"

"Almost. What kind of cop is he?" Camille stood, restless now, and walked to the window. Outdoors the sun was shining, boosting the November temperature into the seventies. There was no sign of Pike Barrett in his devastating new suit. She waited with interest for Alice's response.

"Oh, my. I really couldn't say. I'd have to see him on duty before I could make a guess. He's such an enigma."

"That's my reaction, too. I've seen him on duty, and he's a different person." Camille took a last glance out the window, then came back and picked up the vase. "I'm going to put this on my desk," she said, burying her nose in the bloom and drawing in its fragrance. "And then I'm going to call the district attorney's office and ask Dorcas Wilson to provide me with a copy of Pike's personnel file. I can't put the pieces together because there's a big chunk missing. Dorcas is going to throw a fit when I ask for his file, but he's her primary witness and there may be something in his past that would cause him to be prejudiced. If there is, I've got to find out what it is. Whether I want to or not."

When a copy of Pike's personnel file arrived later in the week, Camille found to her surprise that she wasn't eager to tear into it. It sat on the corner of her desk for a full day, mocking her timidity. It was an ordinary personnel file, about the right size for someone who'd been with the police force for ten years. It would contain all the forms that showed hiring and promotions, changes of home address and marital status, transfers and reassignments within the police department, commendations and disciplinary actions—the bureau cratic paperwork that encapsulated a human life and reduced it to standard-size pages that could be punched and stapled to fit into a neat manila file folder exactly like thousands of others.

Since Pike's personnel file was so anonymous appearing, why did Camille feel so squeamish about opening it and reading its contents? For squeamish she was indeed, and though she picked it up at least a dozen times, each time she quickly put it down. It might as well be a slimy grass snake or a glossy-coated water bug that school children passed around the playground with accompanying wails and guffaws. The personnel file had become something exotic and forbidden, taunting Camille. She considered sending it back to the district attorney's office unopened, but knew that was really no longer an option. The folder was here, on her desk, and read it she must, even though she'd be invading Pike's privacy. She picked up the file once more. At this point, she could only hope his police career was as monotonous and unremarkable as the manila folder.

She started out making notes, beginning with his original date of employment, but soon pushed aside her yellow tablet and leaned back in her chair to read each page slowly, mentally filling in gaps where the official form had no appropriate box for information about personal reactions and motivations. By the time she finished reading, Pike Barrett was much less a mystery and much more a human being. The information gaps had been plugged, but her new knowledge only brought Camille pain. She placed the folder

on her desk and turned to stare out the window for a
long time, lost in thought.

"Are you going to spend the night here?" Alice
asked, coming by to see whether Camille needed anything else before quitting time.

Camille shook her head. "You run along. I'll be
leaving soon."

"What's wrong? You sound like you've lost your
best friend."

"It's this file on Pike. I shouldn't have read it. It's
too personal."

"Well, you certainly know how to pique someone's
interest. Do you want to talk about it?" Alice stood
patiently beside the desk, ready to be either a sounding board or a shoulder to cry on.

"Are you sure you don't mind staying a few minutes? I'd like to talk to someone older and wiser."

Alice immediately sat down in the armchair diago-
nally across from Camille. "What's the terrible secret
you've learned about our nice young police officer?"
she asked.

"How did you know?"

"Why, from your reaction, dear. I haven't seen you
like this since—well, in a long time."

"Since Marty and I were getting our divorce. I guess
nothing has hit me so hard since then." A shiver ran
up Camille's spine and she leaned forward and
wrapped her arms around her torso, rocking herself
for a few moments. "It was his wife," she said, her
words breaking a painful path around the knot in her

throat. "Pike's wife. It was an armed robbery. They were just out shopping, like any other newlyweds on their day off. You know how Pike is, watching every move anybody makes. Something made him suspicious, and he moved up to the cash register to cover some guy who was about to hold up the clerk. He'd told his wife to crouch down by the shelves at the back until he could telephone for help. He was off duty so he didn't have his gun or a radio.

"Something went wrong. There was another guy in the back of the store, but Pike didn't know about him. He was busy with the guy in the front. He'd taken him down and gotten his gun away from him. He told the clerk to phone the police station. The guy in the back grabbed Pike's wife and used her for a hostage to get out of the store. Of course Pike didn't do anything to stop him because he didn't want his wife to get hurt. The robbers got into an argument about what to do, and they panicked or something. The second one shot Pike and must've thought he'd killed him. Then he shot Pike's wife in the head. The robbers made it out of the store, but they were picked up within ten minutes. Pike's wife died instantly."

"I'm so sorry, Camille. That's a tragedy. I hardly know what to say."

"Yeah, me, too. It explains everything, doesn't it? But I was better off not knowing. Now I hurt for him, and he'd be furious if he knew."

"You said he was shot in the holdup. What happened to him?"

"He almost died from loss of blood, but they patched him up. He still has problems from damage to his liver and spleen. Copies of his medical reports are included in his personnel file." Her voice was full of self-loathing. Why had she insisted on examining his file? This was information she didn't want unless he chose to reveal it to her. Everybody was entitled to protect the horrible experiences that had shaped their lives. There were things in her own life she'd want to protect from prying eyes. She had no right to such personal information about Pike. "Oh, Alice, it was so awful of me to read Pike's file. It's done and I can't undo it, but how am I going to live with myself for being such a snoop?"

"Now, just a minute, dear, before you indulge in self-flagellation. What was your original purpose in requesting this file?"

"To see whether there was anything in Pike's history that would prejudice him against Jenny Mayner."

"And was there?"

Camille lifted her eyes to meet Alice's unflinching gaze. "Well, yes, I suppose there was. His wife was killed and he was injured in an armed robbery. Jenny is charged with armed robbery, in a situation that was about as poorly planned, and Pike chanced onto the scene of the crime in just about the same way. I guess his personal experience would make him take a keen interest in Jenny's case."

"Enough to prejudice him against her?"

Camille squirmed a little in her chair. "On paper, probably. But not if you know Pike personally."

"You're sure of that?"

Camille brought her fist down on Pike's file. "No, damn it, I'm not sure of anything right now."

Alice rose from her chair and gave Camille a soft smile. "I've done my job and can go home for the evening. You've quit blaming yourself and started looking at the situation the way you're supposed to, with a client to defend."

"You're right, Alice. You're *always* right."

"Not always, dear. But I know when you have to think like a woman and when you have to think like a lawyer. And so do you. No matter how attractive Lieutenant Barrett may be, right now you have to be one hundred percent a lawyer. The woman in you is going to have to wait."

Though Camille was tormented, the personnel file served as a catalyst to get her hard at work on Jenny's case. Camille didn't want to use the information; the very notion offended her sensibilities. She would have to find other evidence that would be just as useful in defending her client. And it looked as though she would have to start with Jenny herself. There were no other leads.

Camille chose her outfit carefully for her trip to the jail to see Jenny. There was no point in wearing a black or navy "power" suit with someone as stubborn as Jenny could be. Since she wanted to coax and persuade her client into cooperating, Camille selected her new gray suit, but instead of a dramatic red-and-black blouse, she wore a pink angora sweater from her old wardrobe. She brushed her blond hair until it shone, then fastened it back on one side with a black onyx clip. A dab of rose-pink lipstick and just a little rose blush finished her makeup. She looked soft and feminine and almost as young and vulnerable as her seventeen-year-old client.

This didn't fit Camille's sophisticated new image, but maybe it would get the job done with Jenny. *Whatever it takes,* she thought, trying to feel positive about the upcoming interview. Jenny was so difficult. *Please, please, make her be reasonable, just this once.*

Camille parked her Audi in a visitor's space in the police station parking lot and went inside to the jail. No matter how many times she came downtown to visit her incarcerated clients, Camille always felt a little like a criminal herself with all the closed-circuit cameras, guards, heavy steel doors and the oppressive sense of being cut off from the rest of the world. It was a part of her job she didn't much like, but it was essential, so she gritted her teeth and did it.

And her clients were usually grateful. Many of the prisoners never saw their lawyers except at the courthouse. Camille was something of a hero because she made it a point to visit her clients at the jail and checked to see if they needed anything. It was a small thing, really, but if she were locked up this way, she'd want someone to do the same for her.

She signed the log and waited for a jailer to bring Jenny to the visiting booth where lawyers could discuss cases with their clients without being overheard. There would be a glass wall between them, and a guard would be nearby, but it was the only privacy the jail offered. At least it wasn't the regular visiting hours, when the families of prisoners came to visit and waited in noisy lines for hours at a time. Camille tried never to come at regular visiting times. It was too depressing.

"Has Jenny had any visitors?" she asked the clerk while she waited.

"Not that I know of. Do you want me to check the log?" The offer was halfhearted. It would take half an hour or more to go through the lists. The uniformed clerk waited for an answer, obviously hoping it would be negative.

"No, don't bother. I'll ask her when I see her."

"She'll be down in a minute. You can sit down to wait if you want to."

Camille moved restlessly around the waiting area. She'd planned what she wanted to say and tried to anticipate Jenny's responses, but the girl was so unpredictable that any kind of script was unrealistic.

The jailer called Camille's name. "You can go in now. She's in the visitation cell."

"Thanks. Give me about fifteen minutes."

"Do you have any papers for her to sign? If you do, I'll hand them to her."

"No, not this time. I've checked my briefcase with the guard." Camille followed the jailer to the designated place and sat down to face her client. One glance told Camille that Jenny wasn't doing well. Her hair was oily and unkempt, her jail overalls soiled. But the real telltale sign was her eyes. They were red and puffy, either from crying or loss of sleep, and they darted nervously around the room as though there was something menacing in the air itself.

It was fear, palpable and overpowering, in Jenny's eyes. Camille had seen it many times before, almost always with someone who'd been arrested and locked up for the first time. The loss of privacy and dignity, the terror about what the future would hold, the claustrophobia, all played their part in breaking a prisoner's spirit. It looked as though Jenny had almost given up. She wouldn't even lift her head.

"Jenny, we need to talk about your case."

Jenny buried her face in her hands. "There's nothing to talk about," she muttered, as though she'd practiced the words a thousand times.

"I want to start putting together a defense for you, Jenny." Camille made herself be firm, though she wanted to reach through the glass and comfort her young client. "Unfortunately your fingerprints were all over the gun, but I'd like to think there was some mitigating factor that would make the jury be sympathetic to you."

Jenny seemed to pull together her last bit of strength. "Look, don't use those big lawyer words like *mitigating factor* because I don't know what you're talking about. And don't talk about a jury, because there's not going to be one. I told you before, and I meant it. No trial. I don't want one, and some of the other prisoners have told me I don't have to have one if I don't want it. They said you can make a plea bargain with the district attorney and never go to trial.''

Camille hated it when her clients listened to jail house lawyers instead of her. Some of the prisoners had been in and out of jail all their lives and knew how to play all the angles when it came to survival during incarceration. Even so, they were a source of vast misinformation when it came to legal issues and technicalities, but for some reason other prisoners preferred to believe them rather than real lawyers.

"That's true," she answered. "But if you make a plea bargain and skip the trial, you go directly to the state prison. I think the jury will be lenient with you, Jenny. The district attorney won't be. We need to take your case to trial."

Jenny pounded her fist on the ledge between them and drew a sharp look from the nearby guard. "No trial! How many times do I have to say it?"

"Jenny, please, won't you listen? Try to be reasonable. I'm trying to help you, but I can't do it unless *you* help *me*. Give me something to work with, anything. I'm not a miracle worker, I'm just a lawyer. It's going to take both of us, fighting hard, to keep you from spending the rest of your life in prison." But

Camille might as well have saved her breath. Jenny averted her face and signaled for the guard.

"I'm ready to go back to my cell now."

The guard walked over, then turned to Camille. "Are you finished, ma'am?"

"Let me have some more time." When he'd returned to his post, Camille spoke again. "Jenny, do you need anything? Shampoo, clean underwear, money for phone calls or the snack bar? Has your mother been to see you?"

Jenny's face turned vermillion with anger. "I told you to leave my mother out of this mess. Do you think I want her to see me like this? She couldn't handle it. Quit trying to play God in my life, Camille. Butt out. You can't help, and I don't need someone breathing pity and nobility down my neck. So leave me alone and go find yourself another charity case. Guard!" Jenny was yelling now. "Take me back to my cell! Get me out of here!"

This time the guard didn't ask Camille's preference. He hurried Jenny from the cramped booth and headed back to her cell. As Camille moved dejectedly from the room, she could hear Jenny screaming, "Leave me alone. Don't ever come back, do you hear me?"

The experience left Camille drained and frustrated. Now what was she going to do? There was no hope that Jenny would cooperate, now or later. There wasn't going to be a trial. All Camille could do was try to cut a deal with the district attorney, and that was going to be a one-way stacked deck since Jenny had been caught red-handed. Camille would talk to Dorcas Wilson tomorrow and see what kind of plea bargain she'd offer. Dorcas had said earlier that she wanted a long sentence to show that the community wasn't going to put up with teenagers running wild with guns and threatening the lives of innocent people. To someone like Dorcas, a "long sentence" meant fifty or sixty years, maybe life.

God help Jenny. No one else could.

Chapter Five

As Camille was leaving the jail, still shaken by Jenny's histrionics, some impulse made her detour to the wing of the police station where the special crimes unit was located. Several people were busy at work, but they all stopped what they were doing when Camille stepped inside and asked for Pike Barrett.

"His office is in the back," someone said.

Camille was already losing her nerve. Pike's colleagues were obviously speculating about who she was and why she'd come. This was worse than walking down the corridors of the courthouse and knowing that everyone was watching her. She could imagine how these people were going to grill Pike for information when she left, probably give him a hard time in the bruising way men joke with each other. She fought an urge to back through the door and escape before she gave them anything else to gossip about. Her chin tilted forward, her shoulders squared. "Shall I go on back?" she asked in a voice she hoped was sharp enough to squelch their curiosity.

"Sure. He's around here somewhere. Be sure to knock first, even if the door's open. He gets really mad if you don't knock."

There was a chorus of agreement from the others.

Camille felt five pairs of eyes on her as she made her way to the back and tapped on the glass panel of the open door. She peeked inside an office too small for its occupant to hide himself in. Pike wasn't there.

"Not in, huh?" asked a stocky young detective who'd followed her back. His name tag identified him as Officer Gary Fletcher. "He's on duty. Must be upstairs. Want to sit and wait for a few minutes?"

Waiting in this group of prying eyes was the last thing on earth Camille wanted to do. "No, I'm in something of a rush. I'll leave my card and get back to him later." She reached in her purse for the small gold-plated case that held her business cards and extracted one. She really ought to write something on the back of it, something about the flower Pike had sent, but this was one time when silence was golden. She already knew her card would be passed from hand to hand as the group tried to figure out why she'd come to call on their boss. No sense tossing them any other juicy morsels to rip apart.

She handed her card to Officer Fletcher. "If you don't mind, give this to Lieutenant Barrett and tell him I'll contact him later." While the detective stared at her card and nodded, Camille quickly retraced her steps and was almost running as she left the special crimes unit and headed down the short corridor. When she got to the corner, she bumped headlong into someone hurrying from a different direction.

Someone grabbed her, and instinctively she reached out and held on to keep from falling.

"Are you okay?" asked a familiar voice.

"Pike, it's you." Now Camille not only felt shaken, but she also felt her heart begin to pound. He was so close she could feel his breath against her cheek, and they were still holding onto each other.

"Camille?" He seemed puzzled to find her here. "Sorry, I didn't hear you coming around the corner. I know better than to come so fast around that blind spot. You're not hurt, are you?"

She shook her head. "No, I'm fine. Just a little shaken, that's all." It was time to step away from him, but before she could reluctantly do so, he'd dropped his arms and rearranged the expression on his face. His mouth was set in a rigid line.

"Do you have time for a cup of coffee?" he asked. "I've been wanting to talk to you."

"Well, sure. I've wanted to talk to you, too. In fact, that's why I came by your office, to thank you for the lovely flower."

He seemed annoyed that she'd mentioned his gift and brushed aside her thanks. "Let's go up to the snack bar," he said. "We have a coffeepot in the special crimes unit, but those guys will listen to every word we say. It's not quite as bad in the snack bar." He led the way, but said nothing more. He seemed to be waiting until they got to a place where they could sit down and face each other before he would be ready to carry on the conversation.

Camille found herself thrown for another loss. Pike didn't just send out mixed signals, he broadcast a virtual potpourri of them. Today he was tough-guy incarnate. Of all days for her to be wearing a pink angora sweater!

"What do you want in your coffee?" he asked when he'd found a table at the deserted edge of the snack bar and perfunctorily seated her.

"Black is fine."

He was back soon and handed her a steaming cup of coffee, then busied himself with dumping sugar and powdered milk into his own. "The sugar gives me a lift to get through the afternoon," he said when he caught her staring at his discarded packets. "Extra energy."

"You certainly like it sweet."

"Yep. My grandma always said I inherited the family sweet tooth."

"This grandmother you're always quoting must be quite a lady."

"Yeah." He took a long sip before adding, "She pretty much raised me. My dad was killed in an oil rig accident when I was a baby, and my mom kind of fell apart. She couldn't cope with the responsibility of being a widow with a baby, so she took me back for *her* mom to raise." Pike held the cup between his two big palms and stared into it. "Eventually she married again, but her new husband wasn't interested in a ready-made family. At first my mom made promises to take me to live with them later on when he got used to the idea, but after a while she gave up. Didn't even bother to come visit anymore." Pike said the words without any emotion whatsoever, as though the pain were buried too deep to ever be felt again. "She didn't have much grit, my mom didn't. Not a bit like her own mother. Grandma would walk through the gates of hell itself to see that I had anything I needed. She didn't have much money, but she had lots of love. And man, was she full of starch. Just about everything I know about life and human character, I learned from my grandma."

"My goodness," Camille said, overwhelmed by his outpouring of affection and gratitude. "She certainly had a lot of influence on you."

"Yeah. Taught me not to whimper when things go wrong because the world doesn't revolve around me. Taught me to pick up my own dirty clothes and generally be responsible for any other messes I got myself into. Taught me not to beg and not to brag. To know I was just as good as the next fellow and he was just as good as me. But the thing she insisted upon the most was to look the world straight in the eye, never back away from trouble, and never give my word unless I intended to keep it. She said to me, 'Preston Henry Barrett, you may be as tall as that mountain we nicknamed you for, but that's only on the outside. It's what a man is on the inside that counts. And don't you be forgettin' it.'" He took a last swig of coffee from his cup. "She died two years ago. There'll never be another one like her."

Sympathy welled up from deep inside Camille, bringing tears to her eyes. "I'm so sorry," she said, reaching across to touch his hand. "You must miss her a lot."

He moved his hand from underneath hers. "Yeah. Anything else you want to know about me? Not everything has made its way into my personnel file." His voice fairly sizzled with anger.

"How did you know I'd looked at your file?" Something in Pike's expression made Camille feel ashamed of herself all over again, just as she had when she'd first gone through the scraps of paper that constituted the official version of a policeman's life.

"The captain told me the prosecutor had requested it for the defense lawyer in the Mayner case. The prosecutor said you were probably looking for dirt to use against me. Find any?"

"No dirt. Lots of commendations over the years. Fast promotions. You've been an exemplary cop."

Pike's answering gaze dared Camille to justify her action in reading his file.

"You don't need to overreact, Pike. You've been a cop for ten years. You know it's routine for a defense lawyer to check out the prosecutor's major witnesses." She hoped she could brush off his question with her quick disclaimer. She certainly didn't want to get into a discussion about his file. It brought out all her conflicting emotions for Pike and made her too uncomfortable.

"If you wanted to know anything, all you had to do was ask." His anger was undiminished. Clearly she'd hurt his pride, and even worse, violated his privacy.

But she'd been representing her client. Camille wasn't going to let herself be hung for a goat when she wasn't anything worse than a sheep. And not even a black one at that. "Come on, Pike. How am I supposed to get you to tell me whether there's anything in your past that might affect your attitude or testimony in the Jenny Mayner case? I'm not allowed to discuss Jenny's case with you unless the prosecutor gives her permission. We shouldn't even be discussing it now."

"We're not discussing Jenny Mayner, we're discussing my personnel file. And why you thought you had to see it to satisfy your curiosity about me."

"It wasn't curiosity," Camille insisted. "It was my job. I didn't *want* to look at your file, but I had to. And believe me, it was just as painful for me to read some of the stuff in it as it is for you to accept the fact that I've read it. I wish there were something I could do to make it easier somehow."

Camille lifted her gaze to Pike's still-stony expression. He didn't *want* to believe her. He wanted to think the worst of her. But why?

"Forget it," he said. "Life goes on. You don't know anything that wasn't spread all over the newspapers five years ago."

Camille made one last try. "Believe it or not, I'd rather not know about something that hurt you so much." Her voice fell to a soft whisper. "But knowing what happened to your wife makes it easier for me to understand why you feel so strongly about Jenny's crime. I'm sorry, Pike."

Their gazes locked, as though each could search the other's heart and know the truth locked in its depths. Pike crushed his disposable cup in his fist. "I've got to get back to my unit. I have a couple of rookies on duty, and I need to go over some investigations with them." He was all business now.

Camille found herself again toppling in the fast-changing emotional current. She mustered her dignity, such as was left of it. "I have to go, too. I've been upstairs visiting Jenny, and she still refuses to give me any information. I'm going to have to go interview her mother."

"Lois Mayner isn't going to be any help to you," he said, shaking his head. "She's too weak and wrapped up in her own survival to be of any use to Jenny. Mrs. Mayner is another one of those women like my mom who just can't seem to cope with life and don't have it in them to be good parents. Too bad for the unlucky kids who don't have someone like my grandma to fall back on.''

Camille gathered up her soiled cup and napkin, then stood with Pike. "You're probably right. But I don't have any other choice. I've got to make every effort possible. I can't stop until I've looked underneath every rock for some evidence to help Jenny."

"You're determined to go over there?"

Camille nodded, then glanced at her watch. "This is as good a time as any. I don't have another appointment at the office until four o'clock. I can run out to the Mayners's and be back by then."

"Look, that's a bad part of town. Why don't you let me give you a ride?"

There it was, out in the open. Pike had talked about his mother, and about Lois Mayner, as women who couldn't cope. Women who weren't strong like his grandma. He wanted his women full of piss-and-vinegar. And he'd labeled Camille with the sissies. Well, he was wrong about her and she'd prove it.

"Thanks, anyway," she said, chucking her trash into the open container like a foul shot. "But you have rookies waiting for you, and I need to handle this one myself." She gave him a twisted smile that never made it to her eyes. Grabbing her briefcase, she walked across the snack bar with her shoulders slung back so far it looked as though she had a broomstick soldered to her spine.

* * *

It didn't take Camille long to drive through the steadily deteriorating neighborhoods of East Austin to the Mayner address. Her pearl-white Audi was definitely out of place in front of the weed-choked yard. A couple of skinny, underfed cats were trying to find the last morsel in some tin cans that littered the porch. Loud music was playing on a radio inside. Camille knocked very hard on the front door of the small, run-down house.

"Who is it?" inquired a female voice, hoarsened by too many cigarettes.

"I'm Camille Clark, Jenny's lawyer. I've come to talk to you about her case."

The face that appeared as the door opened was anything but welcoming. If Lois Mayner's hair had once been the taffy-blond of her daughter's, it had long ago converted to a brittle, tousled, peroxided mess. Her face had the lines and wrinkles of hard liquor and hard living. Though it was past three in the afternoon, she was still wearing a faded blue bathrobe. She didn't invite Camille inside. Instead she stood in the doorway with her hands taking the place of missing buttons to hold the bathrobe together and gave Camille a put-upon look. "I don't know nothing about it. Nothing."

Sylvia, Jenny's twelve-year-old sister, came and stood in the doorway beside her mother. She was an unusually pretty child, with finely chiseled features and graceful movements. Her dress was too big for her, and Camille wondered whether it had come from one of the city's clothes drives for underprivileged children.

"I put the beans on to cook for supper, Mama," Sylvia said. "And I finished washing the dishes from yesterday. I'll make us some corn bread when it's time to eat." Sylvia stared at Camille, then gawked at her car. "Fancy car. Nobody around here has a car like that. What do you call that color?"

"Pearl-white. Could I come in and talk to you about Jenny?"

Lois was about to say no, but Sylvia's face puckered up as though she were about to cry. "Have you seen Jenny?" she asked. "Has anybody hurt her?"

Lois reluctantly stood back and let Camille enter the house. They sat down on a vinyl sofa that was well past its prime. Camille noticed that newspapers and junk were strewn over everything. How had Jenny been able to keep herself nice and clean while she was living in these circumstances? She felt a new admiration for her client. Maybe she'd needed that stubbornness of hers to survive in such adverse conditions.

"I saw Jenny this afternoon," Camille said, responding to Sylvia's question. "Nobody has hurt her. And nobody is going to." She didn't want to go into the full details of Jenny's behavior at the jail and frighten the child even more. "But nobody has done anything to help her, either. I thought maybe the two of you could give me some information that would be useful in defending her case."

"I told you, I don't know nothing." Lois was growing defensive. She was more than a little peeved to have a fancy lawyer with a fancy car sitting in judgment on her disheveled appearance and house-keeping. And she was downright vexed to be questioned about her elder daughter. Her expression grew sullen.

"Mrs. Mayner, I know this is a very difficult situation. I don't want to make it any harder for you than it is. But you have to understand that Jenny is in a lot of trouble. She's charged with armed robbery and her case goes to the grand jury next week. If she's indicted, and I'm sure she will be, then she's looking at a possible prison term of ninety-nine years. She needs your help. Do you have any idea why she tried to hold up that store? Surely she wouldn't have done it unless she needed the money."

"I don't know nothing about it. If she was in some kind of trouble, she didn't tell me about it. I suppose you're talking about boy trouble. She never brought any boyfriends around here."

I don't suppose she dared, Camille thought. *She had too much pride.* "Was there some other reason?" she asked. "Was someone in the family sick? Can you tell me anything about her motive for robbing the store?"

"None of us were sick. Her robbing that store had nothing to do with us!" Lois Mayner came to the end of her rope and the end of her excuses. She buried her face in her hands and began to weep. "It's not my fault Jenny was arrested. She does as she pleases. I never could do a thing with her. Now she's got herself put in jail and can't work, so there's no money coming in the house. I don't know what we're going to do! It's not my fault she was arrested," she repeated, full of self-righteousness and self-pity.

Camille held her temper in check. She found Lois Mayner's behavior repugnant, but she was here to help Jenny, not make judgments about her family. "Sylvia, did Jenny say anything to you about needing money?"

"No, not that I remember."

"Did she seem worried about anything?"

Lois interrupted before Sylvia could answer. "Leave her out of Jenny's mess. She's too young, and I won't have you upsetting her this way." She held out her arms and waited until Sylvia left her chair and came and perched on the edge of the sofa beside her. Lois stroked Sylvia's face and hair, as though to prove that she was as fierce and protective of her offspring as a mother bear. "It's bad enough to lose one of my girls to jail. I'll not have you making my baby miserable with your nasty old questions."

"Mrs. Mayner, Jenny needs you. More than she's ever needed anyone in her life. This time she's in trouble that she can't get herself out of. Will you please go to the jail and talk to her? See if you can persuade her to talk to me. I want to help her but my hands are tied. Please, won't you try?"

Lois's gaze began to wander the small room nervously. "Oh, no, I can't go to the jail. Don't ask me to do that. Besides, Jenny told me not to come down there. She said it would be too hard for both of us. I sent her my last five dollars. That's all I can do."

There was little doubt in Camille's mind that any money sent by Lois Mayner to Jenny had been provided by Jenny in the first place. Did Lois really think that was enough on her part? Couldn't she pull herself together to help her daughter at a time like this? "You really won't go to the jail?" she asked, finding it hard to believe Lois meant what she said.

"No, I just couldn't."

"Then will you come to the trial in January? She's going to need your moral support."

"There's not going to be a trial. Jenny told me that herself." Lois seemed relieved to have another good excuse handy. "She telephoned a couple of days ago and said she'd found out she could enter a plea bargain. She was so happy not to have to face a trial. And I'm happy, too. This way she can do her plea bargain and get it over with real easy."

"Easy? Mrs. Mayner, do you realize that if Jenny doesn't go to trial, she's going to have to take whatever plea bargain the prosecutor offers her? And there's such a strong case against Jenny, the prosecutor is going to ask for a lot. It's probably going to be a sentence of thirty years or more. She's seventeen years old now. She'd be forty-seven when she gets out of the state prison. Do you really think that's best for Jenny, to spend the next thirty years in prison? How old are you, Mrs. Mayner?"

"Thirty-nine." Camille didn't have to say anything more. They both realized that when she got out of prison, Jenny would be older than her own mother was now, too old to have children, too old to have a life of her own. It was the first time Camille seemed to have gotten through to Lois Mayner. There was a fearful expression in her eyes, and fresh tears began to flow down her cheeks. "I don't know, I don't know," she murmured repeatedly.

"Please reconsider and go visit Jenny at the jail."

"No, I can't. I just can't."

It was hopeless. Camille got up to leave, but Lois Mayner remained where she was, crying into the hem of her bathrobe. Camille picked her way around the littered floor and stepped outside into the cool, clear November breeze. For just a moment her shoulders slumped. This had been an afternoon of lost causes and sore frustrations. Maybe she wasn't cut out to be a criminal lawyer after all.

She heard the sound of the door opening behind her and light footsteps on the porch. She turned around to face Sylvia.

"Please help my sister," Sylvia said. "We've got to have her back home again. Mama can't take care of us. She can't keep a job, and since Jenny's been in jail, we haven't had any money except what Mama can talk her boyfriend into giving us. Isn't there some way you can help Jenny? Please?"

It made Camille furious to see such desperation in the eyes of a twelve-year-old. Children ought not to have to endure such life-battering experiences. She bent and put her arms around Sylvia. "I'll do everything I can, I promise. It looks bad right now, but maybe a miracle will happen. We can't give up hope. Jenny needs us."

Pike had kept an uneasy eye on the clock, and a little after four he left the police station and drove past Camille's office to see whether her car was in its parking space. There it sat, mocking him for his bugaboos. He'd had this strange notion that getting involved in the Mayner case meant trouble and that somehow Camille might get hurt. It didn't make sense that something would happen in the middle of the day, but he'd long since learned to trust his hunches.

He'd said the wrong thing when he offered to drive her over to the east side himself. She probably thought he was treating her like a little kid. She hadn't worked hundreds of criminal cases as he had and couldn't appreciate the fact that he was concerned for her safety. It was a relief to discover that his fears had been unfounded.

Now here he was like a high-school boy checking out his secret sweetheart. Camille had sent his emotions flying back and forth like a yo-yo. At the Broken Spoke he'd been so attracted to her he could hardly conceal his desire, but the arousal of those long-buried feelings had scared him off—temporarily, till she drove out of sight. When he couldn't get his mind off her, he'd taken her the flower, then run away like a frightened swain. Before he could find out what she thought of the flower, she'd done the unforgivable and snooped in his personnel file.

Damn, damn. He'd have told her about Annie when the time was right and he was ready to talk about it. But Camille had pushed things too hard, found out too soon, and put him off—way off. He was ready to forget her, forget the whole thing. But she'd taken care of that when she'd flown into his arms at the police station, reminding him with her sweet scent and genuine sympathy that there was something special about a woman, particularly this one.

And then she'd been gutsy enough to face down a sluggard like Lois Mayner and her no-good boyfriend, Weasel Robertson. Maybe Camille hadn't been in any danger, but Pike had worried about her ever since she left. Some knight in shining armor he'd turned out to be, in his police car circling her parking lot. She'd probably laugh in his face if she knew he'd been obsessed with her safety for the past hour.

What's come over you, Barrett? His grandma would disown him for the cowardly behavior he'd been displaying lately. Running from a woman who couldn't hurt him if she slugged him with all her strength. Why didn't he do what he really wanted to do and go up there and kiss her? Hard.

He found an empty parking space and parked the police car. He wouldn't kiss her because he was still on duty. But he'd call the station and tell them he was taking a coffee break....

* * *

He stepped into the reception room just as some other people were leaving. "Is Ms. Clark in?" he asked the attractive older woman who was Camille's secretary. The one who'd taken the flower when he'd shoved it into her hand the other day.

"Let me tell her you're here."

"Name's Barrett."

"Yes, Lieutenant, I know."

In no time Camille was hurrying down the hall to greet him, a puzzled welcome on her face. Pike could feel the secretary's gaze on them. So much for his daydream about swinging Camille into his arms and kissing her till she was breathless. He had to come up with an excuse for being here at her office, and fast. "Did you get any cooperation from Lois Mayner?" he asked. "I was hoping I was wrong about her."

"No, you were right. Jenny is the real mother in that household. She's carried all the responsibility, and now there's no one. Her little sister seems to be trying to take over, but she's only twelve. The whole situation made me furious. How can a mother be so useless when her children need help?"

"What did you think of Lois's boyfriend?"

"He wasn't there. Sylvia said the only money they've had since Jenny was put in jail has come from him."

"Really?" Pike became an alert policeman. "He's a small-time hood, but a clever one. We suspect he's involved in several local crimes but we never can make a case on him.''

''You don't suppose he had anything to do with Jenny and the armed robbery, do you?''

''Maybe, maybe not. Could've been his idea, but he was nowhere in sight when she pulled it off. I'd have seen him.''

''It might be worth thinking about. Right now I don't see how he fits in the picture.'' They had continued to stand in the reception area while they talked. ''I'm sorry,'' Camille said. ''Do you want to come back to my office? Or would you like a cup of coffee? This time I'll remember to fix it with lots of sugar.''

Pike glanced sideways and saw that the secretary was busy typing and pretending not to eavesdrop. ''I'm working a double shift today,'' he said. ''We're shorthanded and I'm training rookies. I thought we could have a quick bite of supper at someplace nearby, maybe Katz's Deli. I've got to be back at the station pretty soon.''

Camille's disappointment seemed genuine enough. ''I'm sorry, Pike, but I can't leave right now. I have another appointment in about fifteen minutes.''

The secretary cleared her throat. ''If you'll excuse me, Camille, I need to do some filing in your office. Do you mind if I do it now, while you're out here?''

''Of course not, Alice. I'll stay out of your way until the next clients arrive.''

The secretary gathered up a large stack of files and disappeared into the back. ''Don't worry about the phone," she called over her shoulder. "I'll answer it on your line if it rings."

Camille stood waiting for Pike to leave. He knew he should say goodbye. Instead he turned to look at her, his eyes traveling from her silky golden hair to her sparkling brown eyes, and down the soft swells covered by a fuzzy pink sweater. God, she was beautiful, and soft, and warm, and he wanted her. His arms opened and she stepped into them. He took her face between his palms and smiled at her, then closed his eyes and let his face drift down, down, instinctively finding its way until his lips met hers. They came together in a gentle union, her mouth softer than he expected, warmer than he could resist. He kissed her as tenderly as any man ever can, in a slow, delicate brushing of lips, without urgency.

She sighed, and he felt her arms glide around his neck. He buried his lips in the curve of her neck and pulled her close against him. He could feel her heart pounding in her throat as his lips made a trail down its sensitive hollow, and his own pulse hammered in his temples. He groaned with desire, and his mouth broke away to seize her lips and crush them even as his hands moved downward, stroking the curve of her back, her waist. Her lips parted beneath the pressure of his mouth and he quickly invaded, stroking her tongue with his. There was such a sweetness to her kiss that he ached with longing to know her intimately, to claim that sweetness for his own, to make her part of himself and cherish her forever.

Forever? Desire buzzed like a swarm of mosquitoes in his brain, and he fought himself to bring it under control. Things were getting out of hand. This wasn't simple physical desire they were experiencing. Camille was giving herself into his trust, allowing him to take what he would of her. He couldn't deal with this kind of vulnerability, this kind of responsibility. But God, how sweet was her mouth, her body. How could he deny himself, when he'd been alone so long?

She sighed again, pressing her soft curves against his body. Another second and he'd be lost—lost in a sea of desire, lost in a sea of emotion—with no way back home. He couldn't let himself get any more involved with her. If he did, he'd end up with all the pain and desolation that go with loving someone. And he'd promised himself never to love anyone again.

He let his mouth take one last, fierce kiss as his final goodbye, and when he abruptly pulled away, there were tears clinging to his eyelashes.

"I have to get back to the station," he said in a choked voice. He didn't give her time to protest. Like the coward he was, he flung open the door and went flying down the stairs to the police car waiting below.

Chapter Six

By the end of the next week, Jenny Mayner had been indicted for armed robbery by the Travis County grand jury, a fact that came as no surprise to Camille. Also by the end of the next week, she had heard absolutely nothing from Pike Barrett, a circumstance that troubled her more than she cared to admit. How could he kiss her with such tenderness and passion, then completely disappear from her life? Why did he run hot and cold in their encounters, leaving her confused and unhappy? She found herself pondering these questions during sleepless nights, yet came to no solution. Pike Barrett remained as big as enigma as he'd been when they made their first contact at the courthouse during Jenny's arraignment.

She tried to tell herself to forget him, that she didn't
need or deserve such ego-squelching treatment, and
who did he think he was anyway? But something
about him had grabbed hold of her heartstrings and
wouldn't let go. There was bound to be some ade-
quate explanation for his behavior. He was too decent a person otherwise. He didn't realize what effect
his actions were having on her. She found a hundred
rationalizations to excuse him, even when she called
herself a fool for doing so. She was much better off
without him, she told herself. But why was she so
miserable, and why did she jump every time the phone
rang?

It would be easy to make an excuse to talk to him,
but she wouldn't allow herself to engage in adolescent
games. When the time came for them to meet profes-
sionally, she'd handle it in a professional manner. As
for any personal contact, the ball was in his court. She
wouldn't manufacture an opportunity to see him.

So it was business as usual. Camille was busy with
a number of cases, but with the indictment, Jenny's
moved to the top of the pile. With Alice's help, Camille cranked out a volley of motions, including the
standard motion for production of documents and
records. As soon as the judge granted her motions,
Camille called to make an appointment with Dorcas
Wilson to go to the district attorney's office and re-
view all the evidence.

"While you're here," Dorcas said, "I might as well
have Pike Barrett sit in on the conference. You're

going to want to interview him before trial, and things are going to get rushed at Christmastime with people going on vacation. We might as well get it over with.''

"Fine. See you tomorrow afternoon.'' When Camille hung up the receiver, her heart was pounding. She was going to see Pike sooner than anticipated. ''Well, Alice, tomorrow's the big day,'' she said to her secretary over the intercom. ''Dorcas is going to have Pike come in for an interview while I'm at the district attorney's office reviewing the evidence.''

"What are you going to wear, dear?''

"Something deadly.''

"Wonderful. And how will you treat our fine lieutenant?''

"I haven't decided. Would you recommend that I act as though he were an unwelcome bug on my dinner plate? Or after that sizzling kiss, I could at least give him knowing glances and act like he's a tasty appetizer that I can hardly wait to devour.''

Alice's cheerful laughter rippled over the intercom. "Now, dear, you know better than to give a fellow what he deserves. He knows you have a right to be angry because he hasn't called. Give him what he least expects.''

"What might that be?'' asked Camille, intrigued.

"Oh, I don't know. He's bound to be a little nervous about that kiss since he's such a cautious fellow and it was out of character for him. He's probably blown it all out of proportion—just like you have. So why don't you act as though it never happened? Be

ever so friendly and polite, but have total amnesia
about the kiss. That should put a dent in that male ego
of his.''

"Alice, you're wonderful. I hope I'll be able to keep
a straight face.''

Pike was already present in Dorcas's office when
Camille arrived, and she could sense his anxiety about
seeing her again. His gaze wandered the room, and he
seemed to have as much trouble finding a place to rest
his eyes as he did knowing where to put his hands.
During the first ten minutes Camille was there, he'd
stuck a finger in his collar three separate times, trying
to loosen it. Poor dear, Camille thought, his tie must
be choking him. She gave him a wide, beaming smile
and noticed that he squirmed even more. She hoped
part of his discomfort was due to the smashing black
dress she was wearing. It was deceptively simple and
made of wool jersey that clung just a little with every
move she made. Gathers drew over the breast and
ended at her right shoulder, emphasized with a coiled
gold pin edged with diamonds. The dress was impec-
cably ladylike yet provocative. She was pleased to
watch Pike squirm.

Dorcas, who tended to be single-minded and self-
absorbed, seemed to be unaware of the byplay between Camille and Pike. Intent on the case, she
handed over folders and sealed reports with a rapid
commentary on each. "While you're looking at these

fingerprint reports, I'll get us something to drink. Coffee okay?''

"I'd rather have a diet cola, if it's not too much trouble," Camille responded.

"There's a machine at the end of the hall. No problem."

Pike quickly stood. "I'll get it."

Camille smiled again. Inside she felt the sweet taste of success. Pike was so rattled that he wasn't about to stay in the room alone with her while Dorcas went for drinks.

"You know where the coffeepot is?" Dorcas asked. "Help yourself to one of the extra cups. Mine has my name on it." After he'd gone, she leaned back in her chair and opened up another report, then handed it to Camille. "I think you'll have to ask Pike some questions about that one. I'm not sure I understand it myself."

Camille had collected a stack of things to question Pike about. She'd enjoyed taking a little revenge by throwing him off guard, but now it was time to get down to business. This stack of papers was all she had available for Jenny's defense. Somewhere in this unlikely compost heap she hoped to find a clue. She got out her pen and began making notes.

Pike returned and handed out the drinks without comment, then sat down in a chair across from Camille. She took a swallow of cola and looked up to find him watching her. He seemed puzzled. Her ploy must've worked. She hadn't behaved as he'd expected, and he was trying to figure out how to relate to her.

Dorcas got to the bottom of the stack of documents. "There," she said, "my part's finished. Now I can relax." She sipped her coffee and waited for Camille to finish making notes.

"I don't understand these two separate fingerprint reports," Camille said, turning to Pike. "You gave me a copy of one of them right after Jenny was arrested. It shows Jenny's match-points on eleven prints. This other report makes an identification on the twelfth print, but it's not Jenny's."

"Since we had an unidentified print, I sent it to the FBI," Pike said. "That report just came in a day or two ago. It shows that John Robertson also handled the gun Jenny used in the robbery."

"John Robertson? Who is he?"

"Locally we know him as Weasel Robertson. He's the boyfriend of Lois Mayner."

For the first time since Jenny was arrested, Camille felt a surge of hope. "Lois's boyfriend? The one who gives her money now that Jenny's in jail?"

Pike nodded.

"So there is a connection between him and Jenny. I wonder if Lois Mayner knows what it is?" Camille's mind was racing. Forgotten now was any thought of playing games with Pike. She wanted his help. He knew a lot about the Mayner family and could save her time and effort in unraveling what had happened to make Jenny commit the armed robbery. "Lois denied knowing anything when I talked to her."

"She may not know, or be afraid to talk."

Dorcas interrupted the conversation. "Does this mean that someone else is involved in the robbery besides Jenny Mayner? We're here to resolve Jenny's case and see if we can reach a plea-bargain agreement. Anything involving other people is purely speculative at this point."

"But, Dorcas, you don't want to put the whole blame on Jenny if other people are involved. That's what we've got to find out. Can't you use this fingerprint report to bring Weasel Robertson in for questioning?" Sometimes Dorcas's single-mindedness was a severe hindrance, Camille thought. Dorcas would focus on Jenny and push her case to the limit, disregarding any additional circumstances that could be highly significant.

"I already talked to Weasel," Pike said. "Yesterday. Told him I knew he was Lois's boyfriend and knew the family, and that his print was on the gun Jenny used. He refused to talk. Told me to get an arrest warrant if I thought I could. But what would I charge him with, conspiracy to commit armed robbery? You know how impossible it is to make a conspiracy charge stick. We couldn't keep him in jail without testimony from Jenny, and she's not talking. I decided it would be better to let Weasel think he'd outsmarted us. For now."

Camille nodded. Weasel had the same right to the protection of the fifth amendment as any other American citizen. He couldn't be forced to incriminate himself by answering questions asked by a police officer. There would have to be some other way to find out whether he'd played a role in Jenny's crime.

"I checked with all of Weasel's cronies, but nobody's talking. Either they're afraid of him, or they really don't know anything. Did Jenny ever tell you where she got the gun?" Pike asked.

"No. But if she got it from Weasel, and he's threatened her, then that explains why she's been so stubborn and refused to cooperate."

"We need to find out. Will you let me talk to her again?" Pike asked. A defendant couldn't be questioned by the police unless it was approved by the attorney handling the case.

Camille gave it some thought. If Jenny answered Pike's questions, anything she said could be used against her at trial. She couldn't take the risk unless Jenny got something in exchange. "You've been wanting to nail this Weasel Robertson, right?"

Pike nodded.

"If Jenny gives you any information that helps you make a case against him, will you agree to a light sentence on a plea bargain?" Camille directed her question to Dorcas, who would have to make the plea-bargain recommendation to the court. "And recommend probation?"

Dorcas began to argue. She always wanted the maximum sentence for every defendant.

"Then I'm not going to let you talk to Jenny," Camille told Pike. "Why let you make a stronger case against her and have her end up with a stiffer sentence? No deal. You'll just have to find some other way to convict Weasel Robertson. If you can."

"We've been trying for six or seven years. No luck yet." Pike turned to Dorcas. "You know I don't like it when the prosecutor cuts a deal that's too low and lets the defendant off too easy," he said. "But I want Weasel Robertson if I can get him. I think he's had a finger in most of the nasty deals on the east side, but he's too slick for me to prove it. If Jenny helps us get him, she deserves a break. Not a big one, but a break."

Dorcas wasn't mollified. "Pike, I wanted thirty years on this one, and I know I could get it, even more. It's a textbook case, open-and-shut."

"I know." They both turned to look at Camille.

"No deal," she said. She'd fight it out in the courtroom. Now at least she had Weasel Robertson's name to throw to the jury, because the fingerprint report would be admissible evidence. "Ten years' probation. No time in the state prison as long as Jenny keeps the terms of her probation."

"Twenty years." Dorcas was about to choke on her own offer. Pike himself looked grim.

"Fifteen." That was probably the best Camille could hope for.

Dorcas took a sip of coffee. "Excuse us a minute," she said, and she and Pike went outside in the hall to talk.

Camille could feel the tension in her muscles. Plea-bargain sessions were always like this. The stakes were high because they represented years out of a person's life. There were all the imponderables, and every session meant guessing whether a jury would do better by the defendant than the prosecutor offered without a trial. If Camille could get Jenny off with fifteen years' probation, though, she'd consider it a real victory.

Dorcas and Pike came back into the room. They'd come to the bottom line, that was clear from their attitude. Dorcas announced their decision. "The only way I'll recommend fifteen years is if she does five years in the state prison followed by ten years on parole."

Five years' hard time? For a seventeen-year-old girl? Everything in Camille resisted. "Is your offer of twenty years' probation still open?"

Dorcas and Pike exchanged glances. Dorcas nodded.

"I'll have to talk to my client, of course, but I'll recommend that she take it." Twenty years...a long term. But at least Jenny wouldn't have to go to prison unless she violated her probation sometime during that twenty years.

"This offer is conditional on her helping the State by giving evidence against Weasel Robertson."

Camille nodded. They understood each other. "I'm sure she'll accept the offer."

"When do you plan to talk to her?" asked Pike.

"Right now. We can go over to the jail as soon as you'd like. Naturally I want to be there when you question her."

"Of course. I think Dorcas wants to go, too. She'll need a statement so we can get an arrest warrant for Weasel."

Dorcas gathered up the papers and put them in a neat stack on her desk. "If you'll wait right here, I'll go check with the district attorney and get his approval on this plea-bargain agreement. Don't be surprised if you hear him howling all the way down the hall, because he isn't going to like it. But I'll try to talk him into it."

Camille and Pike suddenly found themselves alone. Camille felt the color that had risen to her cheeks in the heat of negotiations.

"You're quite a fighter," Pike said in an admiring voice.

Camille shrugged. "It's my job. You didn't make it easy for me."

"I think it's a fair deal." He offered his hand. "Shake?"

Their hands came together automatically, but the heat that surged at their touch was anything but professional. Camille quickly withdrew her fingers. She was supposed to have amnesia about Pike's kiss, but their physical contact brought back that memory in living Technicolor. She fought to retain her composure, and fortunately, Dorcas returned so quickly that there was no time for further conversation.

"Let's hit the road before the boss changes his mind," she said. "The next plea bargain I take in there is going to have to be for sixty years to make up for this one."

But all their joint efforts came to naught. Jenny was brought with a guard to an interrogation room big enough for all of them, but she was as stubborn as ever. She looked frightened when they mentioned Weasel Robertson, but denied that he had any connection to the robbery.

"You're a terrible liar, do you know that?" Dorcas said. "If you took a lie detector test, you'd flunk. Your eyes give you away. Why do you insist on protecting a common hoodlum? You don't owe him anything, and he can't hurt you. Why don't you tell us the truth and get yourself out of jail?"

"Dorcas, please, Jenny said she's not willing to talk. We have to respect her decision."

Camille wasn't trying to win brownie points with Jenny. She was tired of the battle. No matter what Camille did, Jenny resisted. After all her efforts to get a decent plea-bargain agreement, Jenny had turned it down. The girl seemed intent on self-destruction. "Let me talk to her alone for a minute, will you?"

"I'll be in my office," Pike said. "Let me know if she changes her mind."

"I'll hang around for another fifteen minutes or so," Dorcas added. "I'll be in Pike's office, too. The guard will be waiting outside to take her back to her cell."

When they'd gone, Camille stood and paced the floor. "Jenny, I'm at the end of my rope," she said. "This plea bargain is your only hope of getting a light sentence. I fought hard to get it for you, because it never occurred to me that you'd be willing to spend thirty years of your life in prison to protect Weasel Robertson. This is your last chance. If you'll tell the State what Weasel did, you can walk out of jail tomorrow. If you don't, you're going to prison for thirty years. We're down to the wire. As your attorney, I urge you to take the State's plea-bargain offer." Camille was trying desperately to communicate the urgency of the situation to Jenny, and at the end her voice broke. She was near tears.

For a moment something flickered in Jenny. "I know you're trying to help me, Camille. You mean well. You just don't understand, that's all. I'm doing what I have to do, and you have to let me. Please don't keep putting pressure on me to do what *you* want me to do. It's my life, and I'm the one who has to live with the decision."

"Would it help if you talked to your family?" Camille asked. "I went to see your mother and sister the other day. They need you."

Tears welled up in Jenny's eyes. "Is Sylvia doing okay? Was she wearing a clean dress?"

"Yes, she looked beautiful. Her hair was curled and shining, and she was cooking supper. She's a sweet little girl."

"I don't want her to see me in jail," Jenny said. "Will they let me call her before they send me off to the state prison?"

"I'm sure they will."

"If they don't, be sure to tell her I love her. And Mom, too."

Camille went to Jenny and put her arms around her, then stroked her hair and let Jenny's tears spill over the gold pin and black jersey dress, which weren't nearly so valuable as a young girl's broken heart. "There, there," she said, rocking Jenny like a small child. Camille didn't know much about being a mother, but right now all her instincts told her to hold tight and let Jenny cry herself out. "There, there," she crooned again.

Camille had to find a rest room and splash water on her own reddened eyes before she could go to the special crimes unit and report her failure to Pike and Dorcas. She didn't have to say anything, however. They could tell by looking at her.

"No luck, huh?" Dorcas was matter-of-fact. She wasn't the emotional type.

Pike unconsciously reached out and put his hand on Camille's shoulder, massaging it gently. "Don't take it so hard. You gave it everything you had."

"Yeah. So why does it hurt so much?" She leaned against him, not even caring that Dorcas was watching with considerable interest, as were several other detectives working in the unit. She reached in her purse for a tissue but didn't find one.

"Here," Pike said, offering her a clean, neatly ironed handkerchief. "My grandma always said to keep a clean handkerchief in your pocket, just in case a lady needed to borrow it someday."

"I guess this shoots my image all to hell," Camille said, wiping her nose.

"Well, I'm going back to the office and tell the boss he can forget the deal. His blood pressure will come down by fifty points." Dorcas was ready to move on to something new. "Guess I'll see you and Jenny in court in January."

"No, she says no trial."

"I'll get back to you with another plea-bargain offer, then, after I talk to the boss. Get her ready for something in the neighborhood of thirty years' hard time." Dorcas opened the door to leave the special crimes unit. "Coming?"

There was a tight lump in Camille's throat. Dorcas didn't mean to be cruel. She didn't intend to rub it in that Jenny's sentence was going to be stiff. But why couldn't she have waited a few days before she said anything? Give the wound a little time to heal first. Camille was afraid she was going to burst into tears. She bit her lip and muttered a goodbye to Pike.

"I'm going to get some guys working on the connection to Weasel Robertson," Pike said. "I'll be tied up here for the rest of the day."

Maybe Camille only imagined that he pulled her against him in a gentle hug as she moved past him through the doorway.

"I'll call you soon."

"Soon" turned out to be the following day. Pike had gotten tickets for a football game at the University of Texas and convinced Camille that it was the perfect way to spend a crisp Saturday afternoon in November. The exuberance of the crowd would surely brighten her mood.

He was both watchful and attentive, and she enjoyed the feel of his arm at her back. They sat in burnt-orange stadium seats wrapped in burnt-orange blankets and chomped hot dogs and popcorn while the Longhorns trampled their Aggie rivals. Overhead the Goodyear blimp recorded the scene, and Camille tilted back her head and smiled into an unseen camera, waving her arms vigorously. "Hi, Mom," she called.

"Do your folks live in Austin?" Pike asked. "You've never talked about them."

"My mom lives in Houston. My dad died several years ago."

"So that's where you grew up?"

"Yes, pretty much. Dad worked for one of the big independent oil companies there. He was the comptroller. That was in the days of the oil embargo when prices were high and people waited in lines to buy gas."

"The Texas boom days. He must've had a good job."

Camille glanced away, to the halftime activities below. She didn't like to talk about her dad's job. It had caused a crisis in their lives and led her to become a criminal lawyer. But it wasn't anything she discussed with anyone. It was too personal.

"Look, the team's coming back on the field. Let's play ball, Longhorns!" She reached in the ice chest Pike had brought along. "Good, there's another diet cola," she said, popping it open. She'd thought to distract Pike from the topic of conversation, but she'd forgotten how alert he was to any change in behavior.

"Why are you being evasive about your dad?" he asked. "It couldn't be anything worse than what I've told you about my mom. He didn't abandon you, did he?"

"Oh, no. He was a very devoted family man, as a matter of fact. I was an only child, so he spoiled me. It didn't cost much to spoil a kid in those days, you know. That was before designer-everything came along." Pike gripped her hand, waiting for her to get to the hard part they both knew was coming. "It was his job," she said at last. "He handled millions of dollars every year as comptroller of the company. During the embargo there was lots of hanky-panky in the oil business. Oil was taxed at different rates, and companies were allowed to charge different amounts, depending on whether it was foreign or domestic. I don't really understand how it worked, but sometimes freighters changed their manifests about the point of origin, and there was a lot of outright fraud.

"A lot of money disappeared somehow, and Dad was charged with embezzlement. He was absolutely devastated. No one would believe him when he said he had nothing to do with it. Criminal charges were brought against him, and all the evidence indicated he was guilty. The district attorney made a plea-bargain offer, but Dad said he was innocent and was going to go to trial. The prosecutor said he was a fool. I suppose he was. And so was his lawyer. Because the guy was a green kid fresh out of law school, and the only thing he had going for him was his belief that everybody is presumed innocent until proven guilty in a court of law.

"He believed Dad when he said he was innocent, and he fought like a tiger. On cross-examination at the trial, he finally got a witness to admit that Dad had signed some blank report forms, and someone else had used them to transfer half a million dollars out of the company. The charges were dismissed and Dad was a free man. And I fell in love with his lawyer."

Pike smiled down at her. "I think I'm jealous."

"I was thirteen years old at the time. Very impressionable."

"So that's what made you decide to become a criminal lawyer?"

"Now you know my secret. I guess I'm still as naïve and idealistic as I was then, and people would laugh if they knew. But I still believe in the system with all my heart, and I've got to make it as a criminal lawyer, I've got to. No other career holds the slightest interest for me."

Camille felt exposed and vulnerable from revealing so much about herself. Not even her ex-husband knew about this episode from her past. She'd never trusted anyone with such a heavy secret before. She wondered what Pike was thinking. She gripped his hand and turned to look up into his dark eyes. There was an unexpected tenderness in his expression.

"Come on, let's get out of here," he said.

"But, Pike, the second half is just starting. Don't you want to see the rest of the game?"

"You already know who's going to win, don't you?" He grinned at her as he folded their blankets and made haste to leave. "We've had enough spectator sports for today. It's time for something with active participation." He kissed her cheek in a way that offered promises of better things to come. Her pulse fluttered in her throat as she followed Pike down the stadium steps and hurried to the parking lot far below.

They scarcely got inside his pickup truck when Pike pulled her into his arms and began to kiss her, his lips moving from her lips to her throat, her temples. A matching fire sparked in Camille, and she returned his kisses with passionate intensity. Though it was a bright

Saturday afternoon and they were in the midst of a huge crowd, the parking lot was deserted. Everyone else was absorbed in the game, leaving Camille and Pike with almost as much privacy as they'd have in a curtained room.

Their breathing became harder, ragged, and they wanted more of each other now than kisses. Their hands strayed, trailing excitement in their wake.

"Take me home," Camille said, her voice thick with desire. She pulled away reluctantly so he could start the engine. She could see a muscle twitching at the corner of Pike's jaw as he firmly put both hands on the steering wheel and made himself concentrate on his driving. He moved quickly through the Red River Street traffic, turned on Fifteenth Street and headed west to Camille's house near the shores of the Colorado River. He'd just passed under the Mopac Expressway when static on his police radio became a clear message. "Lieutenant Barrett, you're needed at the station immediately. Do you read me?"

Pike muttered an oath, then turned on his speaker. "It's my day off, damn it. Can't you get somebody else?"

"Sorry, lieutenant. The captain said to get you down here right now. It's an emergency." Static filled the interior of the cab.

Pike flipped off the radio and made a U-turn on Enfield. "I'm going to quit carrying a police radio with me all the time," he said in disgust. "I'll take you to the station with me and get someone to take you home from there." He reached out and pulled Camille against him for a fierce hug. "The second half just got called on account of rain. We'll reschedule as soon as weather conditions improve."

Chapter Seven

Pike called Camille later to report that there'd been a major break in a big case and he'd be working round the clock until the suspects were all taken into custody. His mind was on his work, but there was a moment when his voice became gruff and she knew he was as frustrated about this turn of events as she was. There was nothing to do now but wait.

After a restless weekend of thinking about Pike and wondering what would happen when she saw him again, Camille was obsessed with learning more about him. Bright and early Monday morning she called Dorcas Wilson on the pretext of discussing their wasted trip to the jail on Friday.

"I haven't had a chance to talk to the boss about a new plea-bargain offer on the Mayner case," Dorcas said. "I'll have to get back to you on that."

"No hurry. We still have some time. The trial isn't set until January seventh."

"Say, is anything going on between you and Pike Barrett?" Dorcas asked, never one to be long on tact. But in this instance Camille didn't mind, because it saved her the trouble of working Pike's name into the conversation.

"Nothing unusual," she said. "We've gone out a time or two lately. When I first met him I assumed he was married."

"Yeah, married to his job. At least that's what everyone tells me. He's an attractive hunk, you know, so lots of women have set their caps for him. Wanted to comfort the poor, grieving widower, if you know what I mean."

Camille felt a prick of jealousy. It was understandable that women would pursue Pike. After all, it had been five years since his wife was killed. "Has there been anybody special?" she asked, trying in vain to sound nonchalant.

Dorcas laughed. "From his view, or from theirs? Lots of gals thought they had the inside track to his heart, but nobody ever lasts. He won't get serious. And if they do, it's bye-bye birdie."

This wasn't very flattering to Pike. "Do you mean he's a womanizer?"

"Oh, no, it's not that. The *women* pursue *him*, and he just tries to stay a few steps ahead of them. He's too decent to lead anybody on—but he's also too cagey to get caught in anybody's trap." Dorcas lowered her voice confidentially. "To tell you the truth, I think he's got some kind of hangup about commitment. He's the kind of guy they write books about, or write Dear Abby for advice about how to handle the relationship. She'd say the guy needs counseling."

"Is that what you think?"

"Almost every man I ever met was afraid of commitment, so I guess Pike's not all that different from anybody else. With most guys, though, you figure it's a lost cause because they're never going to change. With Pike you have this feeling that he's fighting something inside himself. That maybe someday he'll commit himself to a relationship the same way he does his work. I guess that's why the women keep trying, even when they know he can disappear faster than Houdini."

"Well, thanks for the inside scoop. I'll be careful."

"Yeah, don't get your hopes up. He's left a trail of broken hearts."

Pike was busy overseeing a major drug bust that consumed his every waking hour and almost every conscious thought. Yet now and then he'd remember sitting beside Camille at the football game, snuggled under the blanket and holding hands like high-school kids while she poured out her heart about her father and her decision to become a criminal lawyer. Well, he finally had his answer to what made Camille tick. From the beginning he'd been curious about why she fought so hard even when everybody else could see she was fighting a lost cause. Her idealism was admirable. But it was also frightening. When she let down her guard and let him see how much she cared, how passionate she was, it triggered all kinds of crazy emotions in Pike. Everything from wanting to hold her close and protect her to wanting to go out and slay dragons for her.

He didn't need that kind of complication in his life. More to the point, he didn't want it. He liked things just the way they were, comfortable and predictable, no highs, no lows, no pleasure, no pain. His emotions were gone, buried in the casket with Annie.

So what was he going to do about Camille? Gently extricate himself from the situation, as he'd done so many times before? He almost had his speech memorized. *It wouldn't be fair to you* ... How many times had he said those words? Yet something inside him rebelled at the thought of adding Camille to the list. He'd never wanted a woman so badly, at least not since Annie. Camille responded to his passion in a way that captivated him physically. There was no caution in her, no holding back. She yielded to his embraces without counting the cost, lost in the moment, ready for whatever fate might bestow.

Was he going to cheat himself out of that ecstasy with her? Couldn't they keep their relationship physical? *Safe sex*. The words were in the media everywhere, but they suddenly took on a new meaning. Pike had to be honest with himself. He wanted to make love to Camille, but he didn't want any emotional baggage. Could she handle a relationship that was nothing but sexual? He found himself vacillating.

Pike signaled to one of his detectives and headed for the squad car. He had another arrest to make. They should wrap everything up tomorrow, and then he'd have a long talk with Camille. Just this once, he'd save that "not fair to you" speech until after he found out whether Camille was willing to continue their relationship on his terms. *Safe sex*. Maybe it was possible.

He was whistling under his breath when he and Officer Gary Fletcher pulled out of the parking lot.

Camille fastened the clip to her necklace of tiger's-eye beads and stood back to look at herself in the mirror. She'd dressed carefully for this dinner date with Pike, trying to pick something appropriate for a variety of restaurants since he hadn't said where they were going. She wore a butter-yellow silk blouse with a calf-length skirt of wool paisley, its cinnamon-colored background accented with a design in gold and forest green. Tonight there were no shoulder pads, no efforts to project a worldly-wise attitude. For this date with Pike, she wanted to be every inch a woman, feminine and alluring.

She'd brushed her hair back and caught it on one side with a gold clip, then added to the jewelry with gold earrings and gold bracelets. She wore more makeup than usual, using several shades of green eye shadow to add depth and sparkle to her brown eyes, a sienna-based blush to add color to her cheeks.

She rearranged a wisp of hair, tucked in her blouse again, smoothed lotion on her hands, wondered whether she ought to spray a little cologne in her hair and decided against it. She almost laughed at herself for the fidgety way she kept redoing her costume. She was usually confident about her looks, but tonight she still wasn't satisfied. She wanted perfection, and that wasn't attainable. She took one last view in the mirror. Was this the best she could do? Would he think she looked pretty and desirable?

The doorbell rang, preventing her from adding one last touch of lip gloss. She hurried to the door, her pulse already beginning to race.

"Hi," she said, opening the door for Pike. She swallowed hard. His rumpled, slightly disheveled appearance had disappeared over the past few weeks, and tonight he looked absolutely gorgeous. Every inch of his six-foot-three frame was in perfect condition, and his broad shoulders were shown to good advantage by his dark brown bomber's jacket of soft, supple suede. With the leather jacket he wore beige slacks and a white shirt. If he'd worn designer sunglasses, he could've been mistaken for a movie star. Without them, he had the fresh-scrubbed look of a cowboy on Saturday night.

"Hi, yourself," he said. The usually serious expression on his face faded, and he gave her a killer smile that stopped her in her tracks.

Her hand fluttered involuntarily to her heart. "Oh," she said. "You should do that more often."

"What?"

"Smile."

The skin at the corner of his eyes crinkled as he smiled again. "You look beautiful," he said. "Not a bit like a courtroom guerilla."

"Come on in," she said, stepping back so he could enter. "I intended to wear my navy-blue suit but it didn't come back from the dry cleaners."

"What a terrible disappointment."

They stood watching each other, wondering where to start. When they'd last parted, their desire was at a fever-pitch intensity. Time had intervened and cooled their ardor, but it was already rising rapidly again. Camille wanted to lift her face for a kiss, but knew instinctively they would never stop with only one. Desire glittered in Pike's eyes just as it did in her own. The evening was full of promise. No need to rush things. "Would you like something to drink?" Camille asked.

Pike glanced at his watch. "I made reservations for us at seven," he said. "Maybe we ought to be going."

Camille tried to read his mind. He didn't dare stay alone with her long enough to have a drink. Maybe he

wanted to savor the evening, stretch out their time together, tantalized by the lovemaking that was now
inevitably near. She wanted him to take her in his arms
and hold her tight, but if he did, they'd never leave her
house.

"Wait right here," she said, and went to get her
wrap, the fringed paisley shawl that matched her skirt.

The manager of Carmelo's Restaurant on downtown Fifth Street charmed them with his heavy Italian accent and his efforts to please them. He suggested
veal picatta, a special dish not on the menu but very
delicious. He would cook it personally for *madame*
from his mother's Sicilian recipe. A tasty spinach
salad appeared and disappeared along with a lovely
white wine that brought a sparkle to Camille's eyes
and a lilt to her laughter. A harpist played beautiful
classical music, and an accommodating waiter made
frequent stops to see whether they needed more ice
water, more crispy bread.

The manager himself presided when the covered
dishes were brought to their table, and with a warm,
Italian flourish presented their veal picatta. He wig-
gled his finger at the waiter to bring another bottle of
wine, then watched while Camille cut a bite of the veal
and tasted it with its sauce delicately seasoned with
capers and a hint of lemon. He beamed when she
pronounced it absolutely delicious, then left them to
enjoy their meal while he saw to the comfort of other
diners.

"You couldn't have picked a more perfect spot," Camille complimented Pike.

"I'm glad you like it. A friend recommended this place. I told him I wanted to take a classy lady to a classy restaurant, but not one of those places where there's nothing on the menu but snails."

Camille smiled. "Would you rather have chicken-fried steak?"

"Not tonight." He reached across and took her hand. "This is a night for candlelight and flowers and music."

Camille felt a tightening in her midsection. It was out of character for Pike to talk this way. He must be as caught up with the romantic atmosphere as she was. She lifted his hand to her lips and kissed it.

His fingers wrapped around her palm and squeezed. "Finish your wine," he said. "The waiter's on his way with more."

"I think I've had enough," she said. It had heated her blood, whetted her desire. Her heart was beating faster now, its rhythm irregular. Another glass of wine and she'd embarrass both of them by leaning forward to kiss Pike's lips. "Could I have some coffee instead?" she said, when the waiter arrived with the wine.

"Coward," Pike said when they were alone again.

"Not me. Sensible. When my head starts spinning, it's time to stop drinking."

"We can go over to Town Lake and walk it off," he said.

Camille laughed. "Pike, it's going to take two cups of coffee before I can even walk."

The waiter returned with their coffee and insisted that they look at the buffet table spread with a dozen glorious desserts. Camille's gaze feasted on the house specialty, Windmill Cake, an elaborate concoction made of chocolate meringue and whipped cream. There were at least four versions of cheesecake, several six-layer tortes, incredible pies, and fresh strawberries with cream. "No, no," she said, "I can't hold another bite."

"My grandma would expect me to try one of each," Pike said. "How can I let her down?" In the end they settled on a lemon torte decorated with pale yellow candied leaves, and had it served on two plates. Camille took two or three bites of a dessert so rich and delicate that it seemed to have been concocted in heaven's own kitchen. Pike ate the rest, his sweet tooth sated at last.

Afterward they drove across the bridge and parked near the riverbank in the Hyatt-Regency parking lot. They strolled arm in arm under the last glorious rays of a scarlet-and-indigo sunset and watched the sparkle of high-rise building lights reflected in the Colorado River. "It's early," Pike said. "Would you like to take a canoe ride?" Camille nodded, and they made their way to the rental concession. "Sure you won't get cold?" he asked. "You can have my jacket."

"Maybe later. I'm fine now." They launched the canoe and paddled in gentle rhythm, sitting at opposite ends of the boat. Camille trailed her fingers in the water as they talked about the kind of food they liked, the kind of music, books, movies—all the things that go into getting to know a person better. They avoided the subjects of their work, their marriages, and anything else that might make the evening take an unpleasant turn. Sometimes they laughed together about things they'd done as children, but mostly they were content to follow the river's current and enjoy each other's presence.

Before their shoulders got too tired, they turned and started rowing back toward shore. The moon had risen, full and silvery behind bands of clouds, and the air grew colder. Pike shrugged out of his jacket and leaned forward in the canoe to hand it to Camille.

"Put this around you," he said. "It'll keep off the chill."

Camille supposed she should've declined, but the leather, warmed by Pike's body, felt so good around her shoulders that she accepted with only a small protest.

"Are you sure you're okay without it?" His oxford shirt offered even less protection than her shawl.

"Sure. I'm tough." She could hear the humor in his voice. "Besides, my grandma would—"

"I know, I know. She raised you to be a gentleman. She'd disown you if you let a woman freeze to death out here in this night air."

Camille tried to match the jesting tone in his voice, but inside she felt a sudden new fear. *Tough.* Yes, Pike was tough, all the way through. Not just on the outside, like she pretended to be, with marshmallow fluff underneath. If he ever realized how weak she was, he'd drop her in a minute.

He mustn't find out, not now, maybe not ever. At least not until they got to know each other better and had a solid relationship. Because if he ever suspected, there wasn't going to be a relationship, she was certain of that. If this evening had convinced her of anything, it was that Pike was the most appealing man she'd met in a long, long time, and she wanted time to see whether the spark they'd struck had any future.

"Camille," Pike said, his voice now serious. She could see only the outline of his face in the moonlight. "I've been wanting to talk to you about something."

Her stomach knotted. If only she could see his eyes and read their secrets. What had brought on this change of mood? She drew her paddle through the water and waited. "Shoot," she said. "What's wrong?"

There was an awkward silence while he seemed to struggle for words. "It's about last Saturday, the football game and all. I was on the verge of losing my head, I guess. It's just as well I got called back to the station so we'd have time to think."

Camille felt herself blushing in the darkness. She'd been on the verge of losing her head, too, but she hadn't thought it was anything to apologize for.

"What kind of thinking have you been doing?" she asked.

"I don't want you to get me wrong," he said. "But I have to be honest with you." He seemed to draw a deep breath, and the next words came in rapid-fire succession. "You know about my wife, how she was killed. Losing her nearly killed me. So I decided a long time ago that I wasn't going to get emotionally involved with anyone again. I don't want a relationship where people end up getting hurt. I don't want to take that risk, and I don't want you to take it, either."

"I don't understand," Camille said. "Then what's the point of tonight—the romantic dinner, and the stroll along the river, and this moonlight ride in a canoe? Why did you even bother to see me again?" She could hear the stress in her voice and tried to speak more slowly. "Was it to explain? You could've done that over the telephone."

"I wanted to see you," Pike insisted. "I've enjoyed this evening a lot. Haven't you?"

"Well, of course, up until now." This part was definitely not fun. She could feel the tightness in her throat, the tears springing to her eyes. Thank heavens Pike couldn't see. She didn't want him to know she was crying.

"So what I'm asking is, can we go on this way? Seeing each other, but without getting involved?"

"*Seeing* each other? Just what do you have in mind? Saturday night dates like high-school kids? Chaste good-night kisses at my front door?"

His laugh was self-conscious. "Not exactly. I want you, Camille. I want to make love to you. But not if there are going to be any strings." He cleared his throat. "It sounds crude and selfish, I guess, but I said I wanted to be honest with you. I'm not the kind of guy to seduce you or sell you a line of bull."

Camille let out her breath in a soft whoosh. "You're full of surprises, you know that? Yet I shouldn't be surprised. You've always had a reputation for playing fair with everybody and following the rules."

"If we go any farther, I want you to know what you're getting into. I guess I'm giving you the *Miranda* warning for lovers. I hope you'll say yes, but the choice is yours. Can you handle a sexual relationship that's never going to be anything else?"

He might as well have said, Are you tough enough to handle this kind of relationship? Camille thought. Because that's what it boiled down to. She'd pretended to be tough, and now she had to continue to act tough or lose him completely. He'd laid out the terms, and apparently they weren't negotiable. It would be foolish for her to think she could change his mind later on. But how could she make one of the biggest decisions of her life on a moment's notice? She was all confused now. She didn't know what she wanted from Pike, or from their relationship. Tough cookies didn't crumble, though, or have doubts.

She squared her shoulders, jutted her jaw forward. "Whatever made you think I wanted anything more than that?" she asked with just a trace of tartness.

"I'm attracted to you, you're attracted to me. That's all it takes."

If Pike was taken aback, he didn't let on. "I hoped you felt that way, too." Then he seemed to think the whole thing had been a little too calculating and businesslike. "Tonight was just for discussion," he said. "We've made our agreement, but it doesn't need to go into effect until later. That way you'll have time to change your mind if you want to."

Camille didn't know whether to laugh at him or shove him out of the canoe. He'd managed to ruin a perfectly lovely evening and destroy all the romance they'd enjoyed. Maybe she *would* change her mind. Maybe her desire for Pike Barrett wasn't as overpowering as she'd thought it was. Right now he was about as appealing as a coatrack.

She turned to look over her shoulder and see how far they were from the dock. To her relief, it was only minutes away. She paddled harder.

"What are you mad about?' Pike asked as they tied the canoe to the dock and clambered out.

"Mad? Who's mad? Not me." Camille removed Pike's jacket and handed it to him.

"Keep that around you," he said, refusing it. "We've still got to walk to my truck." His hands were firm as he pressed the jacket against her shoulders. Acting as though nothing had happened, he put his arm around her and started walking down the path.

"Nice night, isn't it?" He looked up into the heavens. The stars were still hidden in the clouds, but the moon peeped through. "Your hair is the same sil-very-blond as the moon," he said, reaching to touch a strand near her temple. He stopped in the path and tilted her face toward his. "You're beautiful, Cam-ille." His lips brushed hers gently, and for a moment he smiled down at her, then resumed walking.

This time she allowed herself to lean against him. He was so unpredictable he drove her crazy, but so sexy she had to forgive herself for responding so ea-gerly to him. Maybe tomorrow she could figure all this out. For tonight, she wasn't going to worry about it. Instead she slipped her arm around his waist.

Ahead of them, in the hotel parking lot, was his pickup truck. A jovial group, probably coming from the theater, was going inside the Hyatt for dancing or a drink. Camille thought it would be a shame for the evening to end on a less-than-perfect note. "Why don't we go into the piano bar and see if anybody's dancing?" she asked.

"I didn't think you'd ever go dancing with me again."

"Why not? You do a mean Cotton-Eyed Joe when you let yourself go."

The doorman showed them inside, and Camille held Pike's jacket for him while he put it back on. She straightened her paisley shawl, then checked to be sure her hair was caught in its gold clip. They went to the piano bar where several couples were dancing and others were sipping drinks at tables along the wall.

They ordered wine and listened for a while to the bluesy voice of a female singer. "Dance?" Pike asked.

Camille smiled as she stood and held out her hand. "Thought you'd never ask." They stepped onto the tiny dance floor and into each other's arms. The music was slow and sensual. Their bodies were familiar now, and they moved together with a graceful intimacy. When the singer finished the song, Camille's cheeks were flushed, her eyes bright. Her hands moved up Pike's chest and rested on his shoulders. She lifted her gaze to his and saw the desire he didn't try to hide.

"Pike," she whispered, "Let's rent a room and go upstairs."

"I didn't intend for anything to happen tonight," he said earnestly. "I wanted us to talk things over and give you plenty of time to change your mind."

She couldn't suppress a smile. "Don't you ever do anything spontaneously?" she asked.

He grinned in spite of himself. "Never."

Camille stood on tiptoe and nipped his ear with her teeth. "Tonight is going to be different. We're going to be wild and crazy and impulsive. So are you going to go rent us a room, or am I going to start taking off my clothes right here on the dance floor?"

Chapter Eight

Their room was on the top floor of the high-rise hotel with a terrace overlooking the river. Camille and Pike stood in the cool night air and watched the play of lights in the river below. Pike's arm was wrapped loosely around Camille's shoulder, and she could feel the thud of his heart against her ear. She snuggled closer to him and felt his lips move against the crown of her head. Now they were together with all the time in the world. Her pulse was racing with anticipation.

There was a discreet knock at the door, and Pike went to admit the room-service waiter carrying a tray with a silver ice bucket of chilled champagne and two stemmed glasses. Camille watched from the terrace as he paid the waiter and poured the champagne, then started toward her with the glasses.

"To the beautiful Camille," he said, making a toast. "May this evening be even more wonderful than our dreams."

Their glasses clinked, their lips sipped, their eyes met. Camille felt butterflies dancing in her midsection, and she put down her champagne glass. "Come closer," she whispered.

Pike's glass joined hers on the terrace table, and slowly, ever so slowly, he reached for the ends of her shawl and drew her body next to his.

"You're cold," he said, his hands moving across her shoulders, down her arms, to catch her fingers and bring them to his lips. He kissed each one in turn, sometimes gently biting the sensitive pad of flesh at the tip of her fingernails.

Camille sighed and slid her arms around Pike's neck. "I'm feeling much warmer now."

Pike lowered his head and claimed her lips. At first his kiss was light, barely touching her before he broke away, then returned like a hummingbird to nectar. Camille caught his bottom lip and nipped it with her teeth, and his mouth became greedy and demanding. Her head fell back as he made a loving assault on her throat, finding its hollow and thrilling her with a scorching trail of kisses.

Her entire body quickened at his touch, and the sound of her ragged breathing was drowned out by the roaring of her pulse in her ears. Her hands began to move across his chest, down the firm, muscular column of his waist.

Their lips met again in a wild, wet, abandoned kiss that left them dizzy and shaken. They were beyond speech, and Pike caught her hand and led her from the terrace back into their room. He tugged the drapery cord, shutting out the rest of the world and leaving them safe from prying eyes, then picked Camille up and carried her to the king-size bed. Their hands moved in unison, unfastening clothing and tossing it out of the way.

Camille lay on her side and watched as Pike's gaze moved along her naked body. She smiled when he sucked in his breath.

"You're so beautiful," he said, one finger tracing a line from her chin to her collarbone, then drawing a circle around the outer circumference of each breast. Her nipples responded to his caress, and his finger drew smaller and smaller circles until each rosy bud was fully aroused. When his lips came seeking, she shifted slightly and he drew her nipple into his mouth, kissing and nipping until fire raged in her veins.

"More," he said hoarsely, and as he plundered the sweet treasures of her other breast, his hand slipped between her legs and began stroking until her back arched and she was trembling with a need that only he could satisfy.

"Make love to me," she whispered, and he stretched out on the sheets beside her, their hands and mouths a maelstrom of giving and taking, knowing and being known. If she was wanton, Camille didn't know or care. There was only this moment with its urgency of passion that could not be denied. She must give herself to Pike totally and completely, fill all his empty places, heal all his hurts. She opened herself to Pike, and he plunged himself into her warm, welcoming core. Their bodies found their natural rhythm, alternating short, fiery thrusts with long, sensual ones. Their lips echoed the cadence of their bodies, alternating brief, feathery kisses with deep, liquid ones. They moved together as one until desire reached its flashpoint and carried them, beyond control, to the farthest boundary of physical sensation where time stood still....

Camille had no idea how much time had passed before her head began to clear and she felt herself returning to the real world. Pike's cheek was pressed against her breast and he was asleep, his breath warm and even on her skin. Even now her senses tingled at the memory of their lovemaking, and she gently stroked Pike's dark hair. Gone were the stern lines and frown that so often marked his expression. In the lamplight he looked as peaceful and contented as a child.

She smiled with sheer joy to think she'd been responsible for this change in him. What an awesome power a woman had over a man! The gift of her body could pleasure him and bring him a release like nothing else.

But she'd given Pike more than her body. Camille knew that now, knew it when it happened. She'd given all she had to give, herself, her very soul. More than he wanted from her, more than he was willing to accept. She sighed. The pretense would never end. It had been burden enough to pretend to be tough. Now she had the even heavier task of pretending that her emotions were carefully compartmentalized and that their relationship was based on nothing but sexual attraction.

Camille threw her arm over her face and sighed again. How was she going to keep it secret from Pike that she'd fallen in love with him?

In the middle of the night Pike wakened and felt an unusual sense of joy and peace. Camille was beside him, her breath a soft whisper in the otherwise silent hotel room. He shifted and put his arm around her, drawing her against him. He didn't intend to wake her, but she stirred in his arms.

"Hi," she said. "What time is it?"

He looked at his watch. "About three. Does it matter?"

"I turned into a pumpkin at twelve o'clock."

"I thought the bed had gotten lumpy. I guess the pumpkin explains it." He fondled her breast. "Nice lumps." Desire caught him off guard, and he searched for her mouth. "Kiss me," he insisted. "I have another present for you."

"Go away. It's three o'clock in the morning. You need to save your strength for the police department." But even as she said the words, Camille was lifting her face for his kiss.

He licked her bottom lip, then toyed with her tongue until they were both breathing fast. He cupped her breast in his hand and gently stroked it until the nipple hardened against his thumb. It was exciting to watch her body respond to him. Not only was she beautiful to look at, but she gave herself so fully. He buried his face in her breast and drew her nipple into his mouth, feasting until he felt her melt with desire.

Her hands began to stray, exploring his body and lingering to pleasure him when she heard his breath come faster. He took her hand and guided it, groaning as she stroked him to a frenzy of wanting. He placed her astride him and lay lost in a cloud of ecstasy as she took the lead, rising and falling to an ever-increasing tempo. He called her name, and then the universe burst apart, sending stars spewing in every direction....

"Wake up, sleepyhead," Pike said. He was already showered and dressed, but Camille hadn't heard a sound. She opened her eyes to find him smiling down at her.

She stretched out her arms. "Come back to bed."

"We have to go to work."

"At least give me a good-morning kiss."

He gave her a skeptical glance. "I don't think things stop with kisses where you're concerned."

"Try me and see."

Pike sat down on the edge of the bed and gave her a gingerly kiss on the forehead.

"That doesn't count. It has to be a real kiss." Her arms had slipped around his neck, and she tried to entice him with a sexy kiss.

"Oh, no, you don't. It's six o'clock. I've got to be at the station at seven."

"That's a whole *hour*, Pike."

"But I've got to take you home, and then go home and shave."

"I'll swear, Pike, you've lost your reputation as a man of his word. You got me to sign an agreement that we'd have nothing to do with each other except have sex, and then you renege the first day. Wait till that story makes the rounds."

"You wouldn't tell."

"Wouldn't I?" She gave him a fetching smile, then turned back the sheet and stretched out, naked and sensual. "Don't you think it's worth a little insurance to keep me quiet?"

"We aren't going to have time for breakfast."

"Who cares?"

His clothes were already being tossed on the chair. "Scoot over," he said. "I'm not even sure I can rise to the occasion."

Camille laughed. One glance told her he was ready, willing and able. "Just do the best you can," she said softly. "I'm sure that will more than suffice."

In the end, Pike went to work unshaved and Camille took a taxi from the hotel because there wasn't time for Pike to drive her home. But it was worth the mad dash they both had to make to get to work. They spent the day in the afterglow of lovemaking, their senses more alert than ever, their bodies invigorated.

Twice during the morning Pike called Camille, just to say hello. He couldn't seem to help himself. He wanted to hear the caress in her voice, the warmth of her laughter. By midafternoon he called again, to give her the important message he'd forgotten in the midst of all the excitement.

"Do you want to drop me at the airport tonight?" he asked. "I have to go to Washington for training at the FBI Academy. It's been scheduled for months."

"Why didn't you tell me?" Her voice sounded hurt.

"I meant to. That's why I took you out to dinner last night, so I could tell you I was leaving for the rest of the week. I thought that would give you time to make up your mind while I was gone, and when I got back you could let me know what you decided. I didn't know things were going to turn out the way they did."

"You aren't sorry, are you?"

"Sorry? Hell, no. I imagine I'm the happiest guy at the station today, Camille. I look at the other guys and think how lucky I am, and how jealous they'd be if they knew about last night."

"Try not to walk around with a sappy smile on your face, will you? They might guess what you've been up to. They're used to your scowl."

Pike's fingers moved across his mouth. It was true. He did have a sappy smile on his face. "I'll spend the rest of the day glaring at people," he promised. "Pick me up at the station at six, will you?"

"What time is your plane?"

"Six-thirty." He realized what she was probably thinking. "Camille, that's not time enough."

Her laughter tinkled like bells in the wind. "Then maybe you ought to hurry a little with your packing. You're going to have a long, lonesome week without me. Suppose I pick you up at *five* o'clock?"

The thought of making love to her again sent shivers of anticipation down Pike's spine. "Make it four-thirty," he said. "That way we won't have to waste time in the five o'clock traffic."

Even with his rigorous training at the FBI Academy, Pike found his mind wandering to thoughts of Camille. She made him feel more alive than he'd been in years. It didn't seem possible that he could miss her so much. At night he lay in bed and remembered their night together, and loneliness would overwhelm him. How quickly he'd adjusted to the idea of having her sleep beside him, curled against his side with his arm around her. Now they were apart, and he felt an aching emptiness.

He'd been so cautious, planned so well. Their relationship was to be sex, pure and simple. But was it only sexual gratification that he was missing? Was that the reason for this awful sense of loss? Or had he outsmarted himself and let himself get emotionally involved after all?

After class each day he explored the capitol's many attractions, trying to think as he walked for miles. He didn't want the pain of an emotional relationship, but maybe it was already too late. If that were true, he should back out now, and like the coward he was, break and run.

And yet . . . how could they stop now? It was too soon. He'd only begun to know the sheer joy Camille offered him. Eventually he reached what he knew was a coward's solution. He wouldn't decide, not yet. The present was more wonderful than anything he'd known in a long time. For now he wouldn't worry about the future.

He couldn't wait until week's end to talk to her, so late Wednesday he telephoned.

"Will you be able to pick me up at the airport on Friday evening?" he asked. "I can get someone from the station if you're going to be busy."

"There's going to be a party at the State Capitol," she said. "I'm supposed to go because I worked in the campaign this fall. Would you like to go with me?"

"Well, sure. If there's time for me to go home and change clothes after the plane arrives."

"No problem. We don't have to be the first to arrive at the party anyway."

"I'll meet you at the baggage claim area, then." There was the slightest pause. "Camille?"

"Yes?"

"I've missed you, sweetheart."

"Oh, Pike, I've missed you, too."

When she hung up the receiver, Camille's heart was pounding. She'd thought of Pike constantly since he'd been gone, and when he hadn't called right away, her imagination had played tricks on her. She was afraid he'd changed his mind, that he didn't want to see her anymore. At first she'd been restless, but as time drew on, she'd gotten depressed. She knew she was in treacherous waters, living a lie, and that she could be unmasked at any moment. She had to hide her feelings from Pike and never let him guess the secret love she'd discovered growing in her heart.

But for the moment his telephone call had taken away her anxiety. And even better, he'd admitted to missing her. She'd never expected that confession from him. Now all she had to do was wait for Friday night. She'd bought a new dress for the party at the Capitol—a strapless number made of beaded silk chiffon and taffeta. It had cost a fortune, but it was going to be worth every penny.

She could hardly wait to welcome Pike home.

* * *

The rotunda of the State Capitol was crowded with politicians and campaign workers, staff and volunteers, when Camille and Pike arrived. The party was sponsored by several well-heeled lobbyist groups, and there were tables of food and drink everywhere and a live band was playing in the west hallway.

There were many influential people whom they recognized from newspaper photographs and television interviews, others whom they knew personally.

"Camille, you look beautiful," said one of the district judges. "Let's get that television reporter with the Camcorder over here to take your picture. He took a shot of my ugly mug, so he ought to be glad to offer a pretty face for his viewers."

The newsman obliged, and shoved Pike and the judge into the scene as well. He even took time to interview Camille and let her get a little free publicity as a local criminal attorney.

"Let me know if your phone rings off the hook," the reporter said when they'd finished. "I'll hire you myself if I ever get arrested."

At some point they ran into Dorcas Wilson from the prosecutor's office. She gave them a surprised look, then wagged her finger at Camille. "Don't you be talking to my witness about any of your cases," she said. "Or is this a personal matter?"

"Now, Dorcas, you know I'd never talk to one of your witnesses without your knowledge." Someone jostled Camille from behind, and she had to sidestep quickly. "See you around, Dorcas, and don't worry about a thing."

"Let's get something to drink," Pike said, trying to cut a path through the crowd to the nearest portable bar. There was a long line but it moved fast, and they saw other people they knew as they waited their turn.

This was the first time they'd been seen publicly as a twosome, and everyone took note of the surprising development. Camille Clark, dedicated criminal attorney, was dating Pike Barrett, equally dedicated police officer. "I think everyone we know must be here tonight," said Camille, sipping her white wine from a clear plastic cup.

"And by tomorrow everyone in town will know we were here together."

"Do you mind?"

"No. Let them gossip." Pike finished his own white wine and looked around for a place to toss his cup. "I don't know anything about wine, but even I can tell they didn't spend much money on booze."

"They never do at these big functions. Not anymore. The boom days are over and Texas is busted. Not even the most prosperous lobbyists spend big money on wine these days."

"Camille, do you mind? About the gossip, I mean? People are going to talk about us."

"Because we're such opposites, you mean? They're all shocked."

"Well, aren't you a little shocked yourself? Sometimes I think about you, and how beautiful you are, and how you could have any guy in town, and I can't believe you'd waste your time on a dull, plodding cop like me." They'd circled the rotunda by this time and found a relatively quiet spot away from the band. Pike stood looking down at Camille, his entire body tense for her response.

"And I look at you and remember how sexy you are, and all I can think about is running away to a desert island with you." Camille wasn't going to be caught with her emotions showing yet. She still had her secrets to keep hidden from Pike. "It's been a long week, Pike. I can hardly wait until we can cut loose from this party and be alone."

"I thought you wanted to come to the party."

"I did. I do. I wanted to wear my new dress for you. I wanted us to get all dressed up and show off at a splashy party with all the important people. But in a little while, I'm going to be ready for us to say our goodbyes and find an intimate place where we can be alone together." She stood on tiptoe in her high-heeled shoes and kissed Pike's cheek.

"You're still full of surprises," he said, unconsciously slipping an arm around her waist as they stood at the edge of the crowd. "I see you in the courtroom, and you're as cool as ice. Then we're alone and the ice turns to fire."

"Is that a complaint?"

Pike's lips twisted in a grin. "What man in his right mind would complain about a passionate woman?"

"Just checking." She nestled in the crook of his arm as though she belonged there. "It cuts both ways, you know. You go around with that scowl on your face all the time, and then out of the blue you show up on my doorstep with a yellow rose. You've had me guessing a time or two myself."

"You don't like roses?"

"Of course I like roses. I love roses. Especially yellow ones. I just can't figure you out sometimes, that's all."

"Is that a complaint?" He mimicked her earlier question to him.

"Not at all. It's the secret of your charm. Always keep them guessing. Besides, I like that scowl of yours."

"You do?"

"Sure. It makes me appreciate your smile when you finally decide to show it off."

"Like this?" He gave her a phony smile that made her laugh.

"That makes you look like a television commercial for a mortuary."

He tried again.

"Nope. Too wide. Looks like one of those toothy grins on a bear rug. With a dead bear."

He laughed, and his real smile, the one that stopped her heartbeat, lit his face. "You're full of compliments tonight."

"A tart tongue is the secret of *my* charm. Besides, it keeps you from getting cocky."

"Why don't we bundle up our charm and get out of here?" Pike said. "The party was great, but I've missed you like hell." His lips brushed her ear. "Let's go someplace where we can make up for lost time."

If anybody saw them kiss as they descended the Capitol steps, Camille didn't care. Pike was home again, and so far she'd locked away her secret and kept up the masquerade. She was a woman in love, daring fate to unmask her on this glorious, glittering night.

Chapter Nine

Camille sat curled up on her sofa with a client file in her lap while Pike stretched out on the floor, watching a football game on TV. She'd watch an occasional replay, or laugh at Pike when he got too excited over a bad play or a bad call by the referee.

It had become a comfortable pattern for them over the past few weeks. The Thanksgiving and Christmas holidays had come and gone, and the usual year-end slack period had settled in at Camille's office. Most of the judges were on vacation and nothing much was going on at the courthouse. But all that was about to change. The jury dockets were heavy in January, and Camille found herself with several cases scheduled for trial during the first two weeks of the new year. She couldn't afford to waste valuable preparation time, but she wanted to be with Pike as much as possible. So she worked while he watched football, and they made the most of halftime.

"What a lousy game," he muttered, flipping the remote control to see if he could find something better on another channel. "Are you nearly finished with what you're doing?"

Camille smiled at Pike over the top of her file folder. "No. I thought you'd be occupied for two hours, so I brought home a big file."

"I guess it won't wait?"

"Not forever. I've got to finish it sometime today."

He got to his feet and stretched. "Then I'm going to start a fire in the grill and cook supper for you."

"Really?" Usually they went out to eat or ordered a pizza. "I'm not sure there's anything in the refrigerator."

"I'll go to the grocery store and get us a nice steak. How's that for a bargain?"

"Sounds great to me. I just hope I can afford to pay whatever you're going to charge me."

Pike sat on the edge of the sofa and scooped her into his arms, file and all. "The price will be astronomical. And worth every penny."

"Are you that good a cook?" Their lips brushed. By now they'd learned better than to exchange serious kisses unless they intended to make love. Once started, there was no stopping them.

"The greatest. Wait till you taste my home-fried potatoes with a little green onion and chili pepper."

"I can hardly wait." Camille took a chance and popped a quick kiss on Pike's lips. "You know, when I first met you I thought you were married. You seemed so domesticated, somehow. Now you tell me what a great cook you are, and I don't even boil water."

"Weird, isn't it? You can thank my grandma for teaching me to cook and clean house. She had this funny idea that too many guys get married because they don't know how to take care of themselves. She wanted me to be independent so I wouldn't get married until I met the right woman."

"Did she ever meet your wife?"

"Annie? Oh, yeah, Grandma loved Annie. Said she had plenty of iron in her spine." Pike pulled Camille close against his heart and kissed her temple. "Let's not talk about Annie, Camille. That part of my life is over. I've finally quit hurting from it, and I don't want to stir up any painful reminders, okay?"

"Sorry." She sat upright and reached for her file, trying to shake away the tears that had sprung to her lashes. If only she could be honest with Pike, if only she could tell him she loved him. But she'd agreed to his terms, and that's the way it was going to be.

She locked her hands behind Pike's neck, drawing his face down to hers. "If you're going to light a fire in the grill, I suggest you get started," she said with a suggestive huskiness in her voice. "Otherwise, I'm going to light a fire somewhere else."

They kissed, a gentle, tender kiss.

"I'm off to the grocery store," Pike said when he lifted his head. "Work hard while I'm gone. We don't want that file to interfere with our recreational activities later on."

Camille was working alone in her office when the telephone rang.

"I got tickets for that New Year's Eve party you said you wanted to go to," Pike said, his voice tinged with self-congratulation. "What time shall I pick you up?"

"But it was sold-out! Pike, how wonderful. You must've paid a fortune for the tickets."

"Anything to keep you in my debt."

There were going to be lots of New Year's Eve parties tonight, and Camille would've been satisfied with almost any of them. She'd only casually mentioned that she would like to hear a particular band. But how like Pike to find a way to get tickets when everyone in town knew it had been sold-out for two weeks. "When does it start, around nine?"

"Yeah, but I thought you'd like to go out to dinner first. I'll be through at the station around four."

Camille glanced at her watch. It was just past noon. "I should be finished by four o'clock, too," she said. "I have a little work to finish here and then I'm going over to the east side to see if I can talk to Weasel Robertson."

"Weasel Robertson? What's the point of talking to him? He's not going to tell you anything."

"I have to try, Pike. Jenny Mayner still refuses to cooperate, and her trial date is next week. The best plea-bargain offer I could get from Dorcas is thirty years in the state prison. If I could get anything helpful from Weasel Robertson, Dorcas might be willing to cut a better deal."

"You need to stay away from Weasel Robertson," Pike insisted. "He's a bad character. Besides, I've talked to him myself and didn't get anywhere. It's a waste of your time."

Camille felt her hackles rise. "Just because he wouldn't tell you anything doesn't mean he won't tell me. I'm not a cop. He might be more willing to talk to me."

"Camille, please, sweetheart. I'm telling you, the guy is no good. I don't want you going over there alone. If you're so determined, I'll go with you."

Camille tried not to feel defensive, but she was annoyed nonetheless. For a minute she said nothing, trying to concentrate on Jenny and her case. If Weasel talked, he might implicate Jenny in other crimes. Camille had no way of knowing what Jenny and Weasel might have done in the past. And if Weasel said anything in Pike's presence, Jenny could be in worse trouble than she already was. Camille couldn't afford to have Weasel say anything about Jenny with a police officer on the scene. "Thank you for offering, Pike," she said. "But this is my case, and I have to talk to Weasel alone."

"You won't change your mind?"

"I can't."

"Okay, then, have it your way. What time shall I pick you up for the New Year's Eve party?"

"Why don't you come over about six. We'll have time for a drink before we go out to dinner. Okay?"

"Sure, whatever you say. And you be careful with Weasel Robertson."

Camille drove east of the interstate into a section of Austin that was a different world from her own. There were run-down shacks and seedy apartment houses, streets lined with dilapidated cars and children who had nowhere else to play. She was definitely out of place in her shiny Audi and her designer suit. She peered at the poorly marked street numbers, hunting the address listed with Weasel Robertson's fingerprint identification. Possibly he would be at Lois Mayner's house, but Camille would try his own address first. She'd rather catch him alone if possible. She wasn't eager to see Lois Mayner again anyway, and it would be easier to talk to him if Lois weren't present.

She found the right street number and pulled into the parking lot of a small apartment building. She could feel people watching as she walked in front of a group of shabbily dressed men loitering near a motorcycle as though they had nothing better to do. She went to the door of apartment ten and knocked.

"Yeah?" The windowshade rattled, and she could see part of a face peeking out.

"Mr. Robertson?"

"Who wants to know?"

"I'm Camille Clark. I'm a lawyer. I'd like to talk to you."

"Nobody here needs no lawyer."

"I'm Jenny Mayner's lawyer. Court-appointed. Your name has come up in connection with her case." Camille was trying to keep her voice down. The men she'd just passed were openly eavesdropping. Privacy didn't mean much in this part of town.

The door opened. "Can't you keep your mouth shut?" Weasel asked. "I don't want the whole town knowing my personal business."

He was a slender, small-boned man with a weak chin and a furtive expression on his face. His dark eyes were bright and unusually large but darted everywhere instead of meeting Camille's gaze. His thinning brown hair was combed straight back from his forehead. *Weasel.* He certainly looked and acted like one.

Camille jutted out her jaw and hoped she could come across as tough enough to ensure his cooperation.

"May I come inside?" she asked. "I'd like to ask you a few questions."

"Oh, yeah? What if I don't want to give you a few answers?"

His tone was nasty, but as Camille went inside and sat down on the kitchen chair he indicated, she didn't see any reason to be afraid of him. "I'm sure you know that Jenny Mayner is in jail on armed robbery charges," Camille began. "I understand that you're acquainted with her family."

Weasel sat down at the kitchen table across from Camille. "So what if Lois and me are keeping company? What's that got to do with that crazy daughter of hers?"

"The gun, Mr. Robertson. The one Jenny used in the robbery attempt. It had her fingerprints on it, confirmed by the FBI. It also had yours on it."

He stared over her head. "Don't know nothing about it."

"There has to be an explanation. Did Jenny steal the gun from you?" It was a trick question. He'd be tempted to say yes to heap all the suspicion on Jenny. But if he did, then he was admitting ownership of the gun.

"Lady, I told you. I don't know nothing about it."

Camille was disappointed but not surprised by his answer. It would be naïve for her to think she could trap him with one question when the police force hadn't been able to catch him with several years' effort.

She would try to play on his human feelings. "If Jenny goes to the state prison, there's no one to support her mother and sister. They need her, Mr. Robertson. If you could give me any information about why Jenny might've committed the offense, it would help her to get a lighter sentence.''

He shrugged with indifference. ''She got herself into jail, let her get herself out. It's nothing to me either way. I don't know why she did it and I wouldn't tell you if I did. Me, I got no use for cops or for lawyers.''

So much for human feelings, Camille thought. She was convinced that Weasel knew things he wasn't telling, probably to protect his own precious hide. Her instincts told her that Jenny would never have gotten into an armed robbery without someone like Weasel calling the shots. Someone else must've planned the robbery and coerced Jenny into doing it. But how? And how had he forced her to remain silent after she was arrested? He hadn't been near the jail, and Lois Mayner hadn't gone to visit Jenny, either. Once she was arrested, Jenny had everything to gain and nothing to lose by talking. Yet she'd remained steadfastly silent. Why? It was time to be aggressive and see if she couldn't strike a blow that would startle him into admitting his guilt.

''Mr. Robertson, you're the only adult who's had anything to do with the Mayner family. Jenny isn't smart enough to pull off an armed robbery by herself. Don't you think it's pretty rotten for a man your age to take advantage of an innocent young girl by getting her to do your dirty work for you?''

"Look, lady—"

"What was in it for Jenny, Mr. Robertson? Besides a possible ninety-nine years in prison, I mean? Why did she do it for you?"

Weasel was on his feet and shouting. "I told you I know nothing. She's a stupid kid. It ain't my affair. Now get out of here."

"I think you're lying, Mr. Robertson. I think you forced Jenny to help you."

"Get out of here," he said, his face a pulsing magenta. He grabbed her shoulder and dragged her to her feet with a strength belied by his slender build.

Camille wouldn't, couldn't give up now, not when she was getting such a strong reaction from him. She might be on the verge of learning the truth. "How did you do it, Mr. Robertson? What are you holding over Jenny's head so she won't talk? It must be something pretty serious, and that tells me you're in some kind of big trouble yourself and you're using Jenny for a shield between you and the police!"

His hand moved so fast she scarcely caught the significance until she felt a butcher knife at her throat. "You're trespassing on my property," he said, a new, deadly coolness in his voice. "You aren't being smart, lady. Wise up. Stay out of my business." The tip of the knife moved slowly across her throat, barely touching the skin. "Keep your mouth shut, lady. It's good insurance." He shoved her toward the door.

The expression on Weasel's face was horrifying to Camille. The man was capable of murder, she was sure of it. Now she understood why Jenny had refused to talk, no matter how much pressure Camille put on her. She reached behind her for the doorknob and eased it open, then bolted down the stairs. Inside she could hear Weasel sniggering.

This time she was glad to see the curious group of men at one end of the parking lot. Disreputable looking they might be, but at the moment they were as welcome as the U.S. Cavalry. They offered some protection from Weasel's threats and her own terror. She hurried past them to her car and somehow maintained her composure until she'd pulled out of the parking lot and driven several blocks.

When she stopped at a stop sign, she realized her hands were shaking too hard to drive. She lowered her head to the steering wheel and began to cry. The encounter with Weasel had been too much for her. Tears of frustration, fear, failure dripped down her cheeks....

The wail of a siren penetrated her consciousness, and she lifted her face to see what was happening. In her rearview mirror she could see the flashing lights of an approaching squad car. At first she supposed she was going to get a ticket for stopping her car in a traffic lane, but when the squad car stopped behind her, Pike jumped out.

"Oh, Pike," she said, throwing herself into his arms and crying even harder. "I was so scared."

He stroked her hair and tried to comfort her. "He's bad. I just wish I could prove it."

"I should've listened to you," she sobbed. "I thought I could handle him, and I couldn't."

"Did he hurt you?"

"No, he just frightened me to death. He held a butcher knife to my throat and told me to keep my mouth shut."

The color drained from Pike's face. "I'm going to go arrest him for assault. Now I can throw him in jail."

"No, Pike, not yet. He'll claim I was trespassing. Besides, if he goes to jail, Jenny will find out and she'll be even more afraid to talk than she is now."

"Camille, I've been waiting to arrest this guy for years. Now he finally slips up and commits an offense he can be charged with if you'll testify against him. Don't be impossible. Weasel Robertson shouldn't be on the streets. Help me. All you have to do is file a complaint against him."

"I can't, Pike. Not today. As soon as Jenny's case is finished next week, then I'll do it. I'm not going to make it harder for her in the meantime."

A muscle twitched at Pike's jaw. "Damn hard-headed female," he muttered. He pulled out his handkerchief and wiped Camille's eyes, then hugged her close against him. "Thank God you're not hurt," he said.

It dawned on Camille that Pike was supposed to be at the police station until four o'clock. "What are you doing on the east side?" she asked.

"Covering Weasel's apartment. I play my hunches, and something told me there was going to be trouble. I had his place staked out before you got there and watched all the time you were inside. I was getting really jumpy and ready to go pound on his door when you came out. You seemed okay, so I called for a backup unit to keep him under surveillance and waited till they arrived. I didn't know I was going to find you crying your eyes out at a stop sign."

Fresh tears welled in Camille's eyes. "You came to keep an eye on me because you knew I wasn't tough enough to handle Weasel Robertson. And I couldn't. I didn't learn anything from him, and all I gained was a new appreciation for the damage a butcher knife can do to the jugular vein. I was so scared I ran away with him laughing like a hyena to my retreating back." She wiped her eyes with Pike's handkerchief. "I guess I don't have what it takes after all. I'm never going to make it as a criminal lawyer. And you're never going to have any confidence in me again."

"Camille, sweetheart, don't cry anymore. For God's sake, you're entitled to be upset. The chief himself would have a sinking spell if someone held a knife to his throat."

He tried to comfort Camille, but to no avail. She couldn't let herself believe him. She'd played a role for too long, and now the masquerade was over. Her mask had been stripped away and she'd been revealed for the vulnerable fraud she was. Camille sobbed even harder. Pike would never respect her again.

"Do you think you can drive, or shall I park your car and drive you home myself?" he asked.

She managed a wobbly smile. "I don't think I should leave my car here," she said. "It wouldn't have any hubcaps when I came back for it."

"Okay, you drive, then, but take it easy. I'll follow you in the squad car. And if you get to feeling shaky, pull over. I'm going to get you home safe and sound." He gave her a quick, hard kiss. "There's nothing to be afraid of, Camille. I'm right behind you."

Pike followed Camille inside her house, and the door was barely pushed closed when he took her in his arms. Her fear was no greater than his own. He'd died a dozen slow, agonizing deaths waiting for her to come out of Weasel Robertson's apartment, tormented with visions of the kind of harm she might be suffering at Weasel's hands. Her tears had torn at his heartstrings, and now all he could think of was comforting her. He held her close to him like a little child, murmuring softly in her ear until she drew a deep, shaky breath.

"Thanks for looking out for me," she said. "And for bringing me home. I'm okay now."

"Are you sure?"

Her smile was tremulous, but her tears had dried. "I'm sure."

She seemed so small and vulnerable and young. She was twenty-eight, nine years younger than Pike, but right now she could've passed for seventeen. She brought out all his fierce, protective instincts. He tilted her face upward and kissed her gently on the lips.

Her arms stole around his neck, and she sighed. "You make me feel safe again," she whispered.

"I hope so. That's my job."

"But you do it with such a warm, personal touch."

"Only for you."

She snuggled closer. "Good. I'd be jealous if I thought you held everyone this way." Her fingers caressed the hair at the back of his neck, and desire shot through him. When she pulled his head down to meet hers, he took her face between his palms and kissed her lips. They were so soft and responsive that he couldn't have enough of them. The pressure of his mouth increased, and Camille's fingers dug into his shoulders. "Let's go upstairs," she said. "The housekeeper came this morning. We need to be sure she remembered to change the sheets."

"I never knew a woman who had so many excuses to get a man into her bedroom." He nuzzled her neck and waited for the eager response he knew was coming.

"Umm. Do that some more." She let her head go limp against his shoulder, and he unbuttoned the top button of her suit jacket so he could get to the sensitive hollow of her throat. She moaned again, and then her hands began to search out the familiar places of his body, rousing him to an unquenchable passion.

He lifted her slim body and carried her up the stairs to a bedroom that offered a view of Town Lake, formed by a dam on the Colorado River. Like the rest of the house, Camille's bedroom was a combination of sophistication and femininity. It had a thick, white carpet and lacquered black furniture, but the coverlet was a soft peach.

Pike yanked back the coverlet to freshly ironed peach-colored sheets. "The housekeeper gets an *A*," he said. He lowered Camille to the bed and unbuttoned her jacket with fingers that were clumsy in their haste. She began unfastening her other garments, and as soon as her clothes were in a heap, started helping Pike with his. As one they stretched out on the bed, arms and legs intertwined, lips joined in greedy, devouring kisses. Pike buried his face in Camille's hair, fragrant with the scent of sunshine and shampoo and something that could only be described as the scent of woman. He shifted her body so she lay underneath him, and his hands found her breasts, fondling and caressing until she sighed with pleasure. He bent his head so his mouth could make its eager demands, and Camille's back arched.

"Pike," she whispered.

"Yes, sweetheart?"

"Just Pike. I love the sound of your name."

He kissed her cheeks, her eyelids, her fingertips, then returned to the wet, wonderful enchantment of her mouth. As she moaned and thrashed beneath him, he felt himself losing all control. He was as dizzy with desire as Camille was, and there was no need to hold back. Quickly he joined their bodies and thrust upward, driving himself inside her until they throbbed and pulsed with an ecstasy too wonderful for mere mortals. In the starburst ignited by their union, the universe exploded and sent their senses spinning beyond the edge of eternity....

Camille's body was deliciously slick with sweat, and she trembled in Pike's arms, still reeling from the raw power unleashed by their lovemaking. He felt her heart pounding against his ear and raised himself on one elbow to smile down at her.

"Happy?" he asked, smoothing her cheekbone with his thumb. Her brown eyes were glazed, their pupils still dilated.

"I never knew there could be anything like this," she whispered, her voice filled with wonder. "Oh, Pike, I do love you so."

Shock washed over him. He turned away and shoved a pillow between them. "Don't say that."

"I have to. I can't help it."

"That's not part of the arrangement. I told you I didn't want any emotional hang-ups—for either one of us." He couldn't explain even to himself this strange anger he felt, because it was laced with something else that didn't belong, a pride and joy that were totally inappropriate. Damn it, he'd laid out the cards. *No strings.* Why was Camille spoiling everything?

He didn't want to feel anything with her except plain old physical satisfaction. They had great sex together. Why couldn't she settle for that? He didn't want to hurt her, but this wasn't going to work if she was going to get all sentimental and start talking about *love*, for God's sake.

"Sometimes things don't go according to plan," she said softly. "Why does it bother you that I told you how I feel? I'm not asking for anything in return."

"That's not the way it works, Camille. You know that. I don't believe in one-sided relationships. And neither do you. You deserve better than that."

"Are you saying you don't care about me, not even a little bit?"

"Well, of course I care about you. But not that way. I don't want to be in love, Camille, and I don't want to be with a woman who thinks she's in love with me."

"Why did you come to check on me this afternoon when I went to Weasel Robertson's?"

"I told you. I act on instinct. My instincts told me something was wrong. I would've done the same thing with anybody else."

"Would you hold them and kiss them and go to bed with them?"

"I'm not on the witness stand, Camille. Quit cross-examining me." He sat up on the bed and reached for his clothes. "I need to get that squad car back to the station."

Camille looked at the clock on the bedside stand. It was nearly five o'clock. "You'll have to hurry to change and get back by six."

Pike reached into his shirt pocket and pulled out the tickets to the New Year's Eve party featuring the Fabulous Thunderbirds. He felt a gut-wrenching pain.

He'd gone to so much trouble to get these tickets because it was something she wanted, and he'd been so delighted to be able to tell her he'd succeeded. It had given him a real kick to please her. That should've been warning enough to him that *he* was getting emotionally involved with her.

Well, it wasn't going to happen, damn it! He was getting out of this thing right now, while the getting was good. It was bad enough to see Camille turn all soft and vulnerable on him. It made him want to hold her and protect her and never let her go. But it wouldn't do at all to become vulnerable himself. He wasn't going to open himself up that way and get hurt all over again. He looked at the tickets one last time and tossed them on the nightstand.

"Here are the tickets," he said. "See if you can find someone else to go with you, will you? I'm going to work a double shift at the station tonight. It's New Year's Eve. There'll be lots of arrests."

He didn't want to watch, but he forced himself to look her in the eye, even when her eyes filled with tears. He felt like a real jerk, but he assured himself it was only temporary.

"So we're not going out tonight after all?" she asked.

"Look, you're busy getting ready for Jenny Mayner's case. I'm a witness. It's not smart for us to be together right now. Besides, I'm going to be needed at the station tonight." The excuse sounded hollow in his own ears. He expected Camille to recognize it for the lie it was and take her cue accordingly.

"So what about next week, after Jenny's case is finished?"

She wouldn't be satisfied until he spelled it out for her. Okay, then, he'd spell it out. She didn't leave him with any other choice.

"Look, Camille, things aren't working out between us. It wouldn't be fair to you for us to keep on seeing each other. Let's make a clean break, okay? You don't need a jerk like me messing up your life." He tied his tie and buckled his belt. It was time to make a quick disappearance. "I'll let myself out, okay?"

He didn't wait for an answer. He bolted down the steps, his memory seared with the image of Camille clutching a peach-colored sheet to her breast as though it would protect her from the undeserved blows he'd inflicted upon her. As he closed the front door behind him, he could hear her sobbing.

Chapter Ten

The last time Pike had been to Dorcas Wilson's office to talk about the Jenny Mayner case, Camille had been there, too. He tried not to think about that. He needed to keep his mind on what Dorcas was saying, not wonder how Camille had been doing the past few days since he'd fled her house and her life.

"I'm not sure this case will even go to trial," Dorcas complained. "But I have to prepare for it just in case. I wish I knew whether Jenny is going to enter a plea bargain. If she does, all I have to do is fill out a few forms and the thing will be over with in fifteen minutes."

"It'll suit me fine if Jenny enters a plea. I've got better things to do than hang around the courthouse."

"We'll find out on Monday when the judge calls the trial docket. But it'll be too late then to start preparing witnesses. Testimony will start as soon as we select a jury." Dorcas started pulling reports from a trial folder. "I'm probably wasting your time today, Pike, but we need to go over the evidence so you'll be ready to testify if you have to."

"Jenny seemed pretty determined that day we talked to her at the jail. I doubt she'll go to trial. She's pretty stubborn when she makes up her mind. Her own lawyer couldn't do anything with her."

Dorcas studied him with a quizzical expression. "I don't suppose you're looking forward to being cross-examined by Camille Clark, either. It's a little sticky, isn't it, to date someone who's going to turn around and try to nail you to the wall at trial time?"

Pike cleared his throat. He'd expected something like this from Dorcas. It had been a big mistake for him to go to the party at the Capitol with Camille and set everybody to speculating about them. "That's over," he said, trying to close the door on that subject.

"Oh, really?" There was more than idle curiosity on Dorcas's face. "You didn't do anything to make her want to get a little revenge, did you? I don't want the Mayner case to blow up on me if it goes to trial."

"It was her choice. I guess she knew she could do a lot better than an over-the-hill cop." Pike hated being deceptive, but he'd hurt Camille enough. He wasn't going to deal a deathblow to her pride by letting Dorcas know he'd been the one to break things off.

– "Well, don't you go for revenge, either. Just be your usual cool, professional self. Do that and Jenny Mayner will be an old woman when she leaves the state prison." She handed him the fingerprint report that had come back from the FBI lab. "I wish we weren't stuck with this report," she said. "It's the only piece of evidence that can hurt the case. It names Weasel Robertson as the person who made one of the prints on the gun, and Camille is going to hammer that point with the jury. It's all she's got, and she's going to push it for all it's worth. She'll try to create a reasonable doubt in the jury's mind so they won't convict Jenny."

"It isn't going to work, is it? For heaven's sake, I caught Jenny in the act of holding up the store. The victim will have the same story. Jenny's prints were all over the gun. The jury can't have a reasonable doubt about her guilt. It's an open-and-shut case."

"I know, I know. I'm just warning you. Camille will be desperate and grab any straw she can." Dorcas leaned back in her chair and took a sip of coffee, then started making a list. "I'm going to leave this fingerprint report until last because that's the only weak spot in our case. I want to start with our strongest point, and that's your testimony about driving through the parking lot and seeing Jenny inside waving a gun in the clerk's face. We'll build a solid, credible case and get the picture locked in the jury's mind before Camille has a chance to cloud it with speculation about Weasel."

"So I'll be up first? That's good. I'll be glad to get my testimony over with." He stood and restlessly paced the small office. "Do you want to run through the questions you're going to ask me when I'm on the stand?"

"Later. First I want us to think about how Camille is going to cross-examine you. It could get nasty, and I don't want you to be taken by surprise."

"Nasty? Camille? She has a reputation for being too soft on witnesses."

"That's her *old* reputation. She's working on a new one, remember."

"Well, let her have a shot at it. She's not going to shake my story. I caught Jenny in the act. That's it. Camille can't change the facts."

"No, but she can put up a smoke screen with something else. That's what worries me. There's only one reason why she wanted to look at your personnel file. She was looking for something to show you have a bias against Jenny." Dorcas pulled a packet containing Pike's file from her other evidence. "I went over this myself last night, hunting for anything she could use against you."

He glared down at her from his standing position. It made him angry to have people invading his privacy. "I'm sure you found the same thing she did. Nothing."

Dorcas waved him back into his chair. "Not quite. I found the same thing she did. The reports about that robbery five years ago when your wife was killed."

"That has nothing to do with Jenny Mayner."

"It has everything to do with it. Poorly planned robbery, scared kid with a gun. Camille is going to hit you hard with the similarities between this case and the one involving your wife, Pike. Then she's going to tell the jury you're a cop who operates on the basis of personal revenge. She'll say you're after Jenny Mayner because you're still trying to get even for your wife's death. She'll accuse you of bias and prejudice toward Jenny. And if she's successful, the jury won't have quite so much confidence in what you've told them."

He uttered an oath. "I don't believe it. Camille wouldn't stoop to something like that."

"Why not? It happens all the time. Remember the Wheaton case that was tried last month? Same kind of situation. Defense lawyers are in there fighting for their clients, and they'll stop at nothing."

"Camille isn't like that."

"You sound like you're still carrying a torch for her. Don't let your feelings interfere with your thinking, Pike. She's going to do whatever it takes to represent her client, and you shouldn't expect your friendship—or whatever it was—to make any difference in the way she tries her case."

Pike sat in stony silence, torn with conflicting emotions. He'd broken off with Camille because she was too soft and vulnerable and had aroused tender feelings in him that he didn't want to have. Now Dorcas was warning him that Camille would be a tough, ruthless adversary who'd grab hold of the most painful episode of his life and squeeze it for the jury. Camille knew his weak spot. Would she really take advantage of him and torture him by using it?

"Sorry, Pike, but you have to know so you can be ready for her. I hate to disillusion you, but the courtroom is a battlefield and nice guys finish last. Camille's learned that lesson the hard way."

"So no more Mr. Nice Guy, is that what you're telling me?"

"That's it. I wouldn't be surprised if that's why she went out with you. Throw you off guard, you know? She even called me once to see what I knew about you. Wanted to know whether you were a womanizer."

"She *what?*" Pike could feel the color rush to his face.

"I didn't think anything about it at the time. Thought it was just innocent girl-talk, you know? Now I realize she was trying to get the lowdown on you and find any dirt that didn't show up in your file. She even asked me if I thought you needed psychological counseling."

Pike thought he would choke with suppressed rage. It was all an act, the whole thing. And the whole time Camille had been using him. For a case. A lousy, open-and-shut case. And he'd been fool enough to fall for it. Dorcas's voice sounded hollow above the roaring in his ears, and he forced himself to take several deep breaths to get his heartbeat under control again. "Sorry, Dorcas, what was that?"

"I said, the only thing that doesn't make sense is why Camille would drop you right before trial time. It seems like it would suit her purposes better to wait until the trial was over."

"She probably had everything she needed from me and didn't want to waste any more time," he said tersely. "Thanks for the warning, Dorcas. I'll be ready for anything she wants to dish out."

Camille sat in her law office with Alice Gordon, the two of them marking exhibits for the Mayner case.

"Aren't we wasting our time doing this, Camille? You aren't going to need exhibits if Jenny enters a plea bargain." Alice stuck another label on a report and placed it in Camille's trial notebook.

"I'm not going to give up hope until the jury panel comes in Monday morning," Camille answered. "Besides, I need to keep busy. Keeps me from thinking too much."

"About Pike? I must say, I'm disappointed in that young man. I thought he had more character."

Heartbroken though Camille was, she couldn't bear to have anyone else speak ill of Pike. "There's nothing wrong with his character, Alice. He made it plain from the beginning that he didn't want to get emotionally involved with me. I'm the one who broke the rules."

"It was a one-sided set of rules if you ask me."

"I didn't ask you, Alice."

They exchanged wry smiles.

"All right, dear, I understand. You're still in love with him." Alice seemed about to say more, then stopped herself.

They worked in silence for a while longer, and Camille found she couldn't get her mind off Pike. She hadn't seen him since New Year's Eve when he'd left her weeping in the bed where they'd just made love. She'd cried herself to sleep almost every night since, but nothing had changed. When would she ever learn her lesson? She had some kind of fatal flaw that attracted her to men who wanted strong, tough women, and when they learned that she was no more solid than putty, they rejected her. First Marty, now Pike.

All that silly concern she'd had with externals—the shoulder pads, the brassy manner, the jutting chin—had only showed her up for the fake she was. Nothing could change her inner core, that part of her that was too emotional, too soft and yielding. It had cost her dearly, that weakness of hers. It had first ruined her marriage, then destroyed her relationship with Pike. There was only one other thing she really cared about, and that was her career as a criminal lawyer. Was it going to cost her that as well?

"I've got to find a way to defend Jenny Mayner," she said, more to herself than to Alice. "This case is the turning point in my career. If I can't help Jenny, I might as well admit that I'm in the wrong line of work."

"Don't you think you're overreacting, dear? After all, Jenny's case would present problems to the best criminal lawyer in town."

"I know, Alice. It *is* a tough case. But it's time for me to face facts. Just because I want to be a criminal lawyer doesn't mean I have the aptitude for it. Maybe I'd be better off doing something I'm more suited to."

"And what might that be?"

"Marty used to suggest I go into probate law, but I never could see myself making property inventories for dead people. Maybe I could work myself into the entertainment law field. That would be sort of glamorous, don't you think?"

"Certainly. You could mix and mingle with football players and New Wave bands. I'm sure you'd love drawing up contracts for them to promote antacid tablets on television."

Camille shot a glance at Alice and found she was smiling. "I take it you're not too interested in typing up advertising contracts for a living?"

"I'm really not, dear, and that's the truth. I'd probably trot my old bones down the street to another criminal law office. That's my calling, and I suppose there's nothing to do but stick with it."

"I always felt that it was my calling, too. But somehow I thought I was going to be better at it. When I was a kid, I used to lie awake at night and imagine myself in a courtroom defending someone. And I was dynamite! I won every case. The real world has turned out to be a whole lot different from my childhood dreams."

Alice gathered up the marked exhibits and placed each one in its proper place, ready for trial. "You know, dear, you really are awfully hard on yourself. It takes time to learn the ropes and get the experience you need. You've only been practicing law for three years."

"Thanks for trying to console me, Alice. It helps." But in her heart Camille knew she'd reached a career crisis. If things didn't turn around for her soon, she'd have to admit defeat.

"If you forget everything else, Camille, remember this. Don't ever give up on your dreams. You've spent your life planning to be a criminal lawyer. A *good* criminal lawyer. If you let go of that dream and settle for something less, life will never be the same for you again. The sky will never be as blue, the sun will never be as bright. And there won't be any more rainbows after a storm. Don't trade your dreams for a handful of dust."

There was a catch in Alice's voice, and Camille suspected she was speaking from personal experience. "Is there a story you haven't told me?" she asked.

"Yes, but we'll save that for another day. For now, we're going to work on seeing to it that *your* dreams come true. So where do we start?"

"Oh, it's a piece of cake. All I have to do is get Jenny to agree to go to trial, and then somehow I have

to pull a rabbit out of a hat so we win her case." There
was a glum expression on her face. "Jenny refuses to
change her mind, so I'm licked before I start."

"Now, Camille, it can't be that hopeless. Maybe
you've been using the wrong approach with Jenny, by
talking about what's going to happen to *her* if she
doesn't go to trial. That hasn't worked, so apparently
she doesn't care about herself. Isn't there something
else you can try?"

With Alice's question, something clicked in Camille's brain. "Of course! Alice, you're a genius. Remind me to give you a raise." She tossed aside the
folder in her hand and grabbed her purse and jacket.
"I'll be back later," she said. "I'm on my way to see
Lois Mayner."

"I told you before, the answer is no." Lois Mayner
was even more agitated than she'd been the first time
Camille came to visit her. At least this time she was
dressed instead of wearing a bathrobe. She tugged at
a loose thread in her sweater. "I can't go to the jail and
talk to Jenny. She doesn't want me there."

"Jenny is too confused to know what's best for
her." Camille was fighting to remain patient and per-
suasive. It would be better if Lois would agree will-
ingly to help her daughter. Camille didn't want to push
her into a corner unless she absolutely had to. "You're
the only one who can help her, Mrs. Mayner."

"No, no—you don't understand. I've never been
able to get her to do anything she didn't want to do.

She just goes her own way and nobody can do anything about it.''

"Mrs. Mayner, you don't want Jenny to be in the state prison until she's forty-seven years old, do you?''

There was a telltale tremor of Lois's bottom lip. "No.''

"She'll be old and bitter, and you may not even be alive by the time she gets out. What if you never get to see your daughter free again, Mrs. Mayner?''

"Don't, please don't.'' Lois had begun to cry. "I love Jenny, I really do. But I can't help her. Don't you understand that? If I go to the jail when she told me not to, she's going to get mad.''

"Isn't it worth having her mad at you for a little while if it keeps her from spending thirty years in prison?''

Lois shrugged and evaded Camille's penetrating gaze.

"Mrs. Mayner, I think Weasel Robertson has threatened Jenny and that's why she won't talk.''

Lois sucked in her breath. "Oh, no, you're wrong. Why, Jenny and Weasel, they haven't even seen each other in months.''

Camille moved in relentlessly. "I suspect Weasel Robertson may have threatened you, too.''

Lois shook her head rapidly back and forth. "No,'' she said, "he wouldn't do that.''

"I don't know what he's using against Jenny, but I'm sure he'll stop at nothing.''

Lois continued to shake her head, her eyes widening in fear.

"Mrs. Mayner, Jenny needs your help. I'd like for you to help her voluntarily. If Weasel Robertson was involved in this robbery, he deserves to be punished for it. You shouldn't protect him at your daughter's expense."

Camille had backed Lois into a corner, but Lois didn't have much strength for a fight. "Stay out of our business," she whined.

"I can't. I have a job to do. And I can't do it without you."

"I told you before, the answer is no. Now please, just get out of here and leave me alone."

Camille sat tight and stared deep into Lois's eyes. She was about to run a desperate bluff. "Mrs. Mayner, you leave me no other choice. I *have* to have your help. I'm going to have you subpoenaed to testify in court about Jenny and why she might have committed the crime. Either she did it because the family needed money, or she did it because Weasel Robertson somehow forced her to do it. I'll let you try to explain it in court." The tension in the room rose to an intolerable level. Camille picked up her purse and car keys, then stood to go. "Call me if you change your mind."

She'd turned the doorknob when Lois Mayner cried, "I'll do it. I'll talk to Jenny."

"Come on then, let's go to the jail."

"Right now?"

Camille wouldn't give her a chance to change her mind. "Now. You want to be back home when your other daughter comes home from school, don't you?"

"I need to change my clothes."

"You're fine." Still Lois sat on the sofa, her head between her hands. Camille went to her and placed a hand gently on her shoulder. "You're doing the right thing, Mrs. Mayner. A good mother helps her child in trouble."

Lois let out a long, shaky breath. "She's going to be mad when she sees me."

"I told you to leave my mom out of this." Shame and anger were equal contenders in Jenny's crimson face. "I didn't want her to see me like this."

"Jenny, baby." Tears spilled down Lois Mayner's cheeks.

"I'm not a baby, Mom. I'm okay. Don't worry about me." Jenny shot Camille a furious look. "This is all going to be over with on Monday. I'll go to court and enter my plea, and that's it."

"Jenny, Camille thinks you should go to trial. She says you're bound to get a lighter sentence than thirty years."

"She's only guessing. Nobody knows what a jury will do. They could give me ninety-nine years if they took a mind to." Jenny's gaze roamed over the cramped visiting booth, everywhere but at her mother, who continued to weep softly.

"If you'll tell them why you committed the robbery," Camille said with all the confidence she could muster, "you have a good chance of getting off with fifteen or twenty years and maybe getting probation. A jury will be sympathetic to a seventeen-year-old girl."

"We need you, Jenny. Sylvia and me, we need you. If there's a chance the jury would give you probation—"

"No. I'm not going to tell the jury anything. Don't listen to Camille, Mom. I know what I'm doing."

"Please, Jenny..."

"No, Mom. Don't you start picking on me, too. It's bad enough already."

"Thirty years is too long, Jenny. You've only been in jail for two months and look at you."

Jenny's shoulders sagged and some of the fight went out of her. "Jail's not exactly a Sunday school picnic."

"Why did you do it, Jenny?"

Camille's interest was whetted by Lois's question. The mother honestly didn't seem to know what had happened.

"I don't know," Jenny mumbled. "Pretty stupid, I guess."

A guard stepped over to the booth. "Time's up," he said.

"Jenny, please think things over. You need to listen to your lawyer."

Jenny stubbornly shook her head. "No way. I wish you hadn't come, Mom. I don't want you worrying about me, okay?"

Camille stood to go. "If you change your mind, tell the guards you need to telephone me. Anytime, even if it's the middle of the night."

"I'm not going to change my mind. Now go away and stay away, will you?"

Jenny spread her fingers on the window of the visiting booth, and Lois did the same. It was the closest they could come to touching each other. Jenny looked so small and helpless it brought tears to Camille's eyes.

"Bye, Jenny."

"I love you, Mom."

"I love you, too, Jenny." Lois moved one hand to her face and brushed away tears. "Don't be like me, Jenny. Don't be a quitter. I should've been a better mother to you, but I was too weak. You be strong, you hear me? Be strong for both of us."

Chapter Eleven

The courthouse was a hubbub of activity on Monday morning. Almost all the judges had trial dockets ready to commence, requiring large numbers of potential jurors as well as attorneys, clients and witnesses. The coffee machines were doing a booming business.

Camille arrived early, hoping to have one last chance to talk to Jenny before her case was called. The prisoners whose cases were set for trial today would be transported from the jail in a group. Camille sat on a wooden bench in the hallway and watched for them to get off the elevator.

"Hey, Camille," said one of the bailiffs who passed by. "You've got a message to call Dorcas Wilson. She wants to talk to you before the judge starts calling the docket.''

"Thanks," she said, hurrying to a telephone. Why would Dorcas be calling at the last minute? Probably she wanted to know whether she would need to have her witnesses in the courtroom ready for trial, or whether she could let them go.

"Is Jenny Mayner still going to enter a plea?" Dorcas asked when Camille got through to her at the district attorney's office.

"As far as I know. That's what she said on Friday."

"That's what I figured. I told my witnesses I was probably wasting their time by having them show up this morning, but better safe than sorry."

"Do what you think best about dismissing them now." Camille hoped Dorcas would at least mention Pike's name, maybe say what time he was due at the courthouse. "Is that why you wanted me to call you?"

"No, it's something else. I've been talking to the boss about your client. The police department still wants to make a case against Weasel Robertson if there's any way to do it. The boss authorized me to make you a new plea-bargain offer. If Jenny will give State's evidence against Weasel Robertson, we'll cut her a great deal. Ten years' probation. No hard time. What do you say?"

Camille couldn't hold back a rising sense of euphoria. Ten years' probation! It was better than anything she'd ever hoped for. Surely Jenny would take it . . . or would she? Camille hadn't known what the final results would be from her visit to the jail on Friday with Lois Mayner. Jenny had had a long weekend to think things over, but there was no telling what was going on in her mind. "I can't speak for my client, Dorcas, but it sounds like a good offer to me. I'll talk to her when they bring her over from the jail."

"All right. I'm on my way to the courthouse now. I've got to meet some witnesses on the second floor, and then I'll come and find you." There was a brief pause. "Tell Jenny this is her last chance. It doesn't get any better than this."

"But there's a catch. She has to testify against Weasel Robertson. What if she won't do it?"

"If she turns it down, all deals are off."

"You mean your offer of thirty years in prison?"

"Right. We've scratched that deal. Either she takes the ten and testifies against Weasel, or she goes to the slammer for forty years."

"Dorcas, that isn't fair. You offered her a plea bargain of thirty years and she said she'd take it."

"Yeah, but I didn't know we were going to cut her a sweet deal like this one. Ten years, Camille. Can you believe the boss went for that? Oops, my other line is ringing. Gotta run." The line went dead.

Camille replaced the receiver at the pay telephone and walked back to the bench where she'd left her briefcase. There were always last-minute surprises at trial time, but this was just about the biggest one she'd ever been handed. Jenny would be a fool to turn down this new offer, but her client had been pretty consistent about disregarding her own best interests so far.

"Jenny," she called, as a group of prisoners got off the elevator with their guards. Jenny looked better today. She'd shampooed her hair and put on some makeup. She was wearing a simple skirt and blouse, but it was a vast improvement over her jail fatigues. "Let's go into this jury room and talk for a few minutes."

The bailiff remained standing at the door while Camille drew Jenny inside the empty jury room and explained the new plea-bargain offer.

"No. I have nothing to say about Weasel Robertson. No deal."

"Look, Jenny, I don't know how to tell you this, but they've changed their minds in the district attorney's office. The old deal is off."

"Changed their minds? What do you mean?" Any sullenness Jenny had displayed was gone instantly. She was alert, tense.

"They want forty years, not thirty."

"Forty years? That's not fair." The shrill note of fear edged her voice. "They can't do this to me. We had a deal."

"Jenny, I'm sorry. It isn't fair, but there's nothing we can do about it."

"Why are they double-crossing me?"

"I'm sure it's to put pressure on you so you'll testify against Weasel Robertson. They're playing hardball."

Jenny's expression was stricken. "So that's it? Either testify against him or go to prison for forty years?" For the first time, Jenny's firm resolve broke. "I can't handle it. Not forty years. Do you know what it's like being locked up? I won't last forty years." She put her head down on the jury table and began to cry.

Camille got up and walked around the table to put her hand on Jenny's shoulder. "You have one other option, Jenny. You can go to trial. You can take your chances with a jury."

Slowly Jenny lifted her head and wiped the tears from her eyes. "Tell me what will happen if we try the case," she said.

Camille sat at the counsel table with Jenny beside her. Across from them and facing the judge sat Dorcas Wilson at the other counsel table. On the benches behind them sat a group of spectators composed mostly of lawyers and witnesses. Camille had caught a glimpse of Pike in the group and had had to fight down the flood of emotions that washed over her. She was here to try Jenny's case, not hang her own broken heart out to dry.

The judge called the docket number of Jenny's case, the first one up. Camille stood and gestured for Jenny to rise with her.

"The State is ready to proceed," Dorcas said. She turned to Camille and waited for a response. Camille had come out of her conference too late to notify

Dorcas that Jenny had decided to refuse the new plea-bargain offer.

"The defense is present and ready to proceed," Camille said. "The defendant requests a trial by jury."

There was a stunned expression on Dorcas's face.

"Very well," said Judge Michelsohn. "The clerk will call a jury panel to the courtroom. We'll begin jury selection in five minutes. How long do you estimate this trial will last?"

"Two days, possibly less," Dorcas answered. "Depending on how long it takes to select a jury."

Camille nodded in agreement, then sat back down. The formalities of the courtroom required attorneys to stand when addressing the judge and otherwise to sit.

"Parties involved in the remaining cases on the trial docket are dismissed at this time, subject to recall at the conclusion of this case." Judge Michelsohn gave the standard instructions to the spectators in the courtroom. "Attorneys are reminded to check with the court clerk on a daily basis. As you know, cases sometimes finish sooner than anticipated." The judge waited for the courtroom to clear of everybody except those involved in the Mayner case. "Now," said the judge, "while we wait for the jury panel to arrive, we might as well swear in the witnesses in this case. Will you stand and raise your right hands?"

Camille glanced over her shoulder. Pike and several other police officers were standing for the oath, as well as the man who was the victim of the holdup.

There were no witnesses to testify for Jenny. Camille would have to make Jenny's case by using the State's witnesses. It was going to be nip and tuck.

In this case, though, what really mattered was not the first phase of trial, when the jury would find Jenny either guilty or not guilty. There was no question they would find her guilty. What counted was the second phase, when the jury would assess punishment. If Camille could make the State look bad in the first part of the trial, and appeal to the jury's sympathy with Jenny's youth, the punishment should be lighter. That was Camille's plan.

She reached out to grip Jenny's hand and discovered her client's fingers were ice-cold. There was nothing quite so frightening as that first moment of a trial when the defendant had to face the judge and the witnesses. "It's okay," she whispered, as much to reassure herself as to reassure Jenny. "It's going to be okay."

Jury selection took most of the morning. They started with fifty people, but one by one they were whittled away. Anyone who had any possible bias was eliminated, and finally twelve people, five women and seven men, were sworn in as the trial jury. Camille studied the men on the panel very carefully. Experience had proven that men jurors tended to go easier on a female defendant than women jurors did. Several of the men were old enough to be Jenny's father. That was good. Older men tended to feel protective toward female defendants. This was one time Camille would've been happy to have a jury composed of twelve grandfathers.

"It's nearly noon," Judge Michelsohn said when the clerk had administered the oath to the jury panel. "I'm going to dismiss you for lunch and request that you be back in the courtroom at one o'clock. Ms. Wilson, be ready to proceed with your first witness at that time. Court is now in recess." Almost before the people in the courtroom could get to their feet, the judge had disappeared through a side exit near the bench.

The bailiff came and took Jenny into custody for the recess, and Dorcas Wilson signaled to Pike and the other witnesses to meet her back at her office. Before she, too, hurried away, she came over where Camille was putting her trial materials in an orderly stack.

"Doesn't your client have good sense?" she asked, still finding it hard to believe that Jenny had turned down her plea-bargain offer. "It's stupid to take time trying this case when she could walk out of here right now with ten years' probation."

"Not unless she agreed to testify against Weasel Robertson. She's not willing to do that."

"Too bad. It was a sweet deal."

"Jenny didn't see it that way. Not when you jerked the rug on your previous offer and left her facing forty years. She decided to take her chances with the jury rather than agree to that harsh a sentence."

"By the time I get through putting on my case, forty years may look pretty good to her. This is the most solid case they've given me since I went to work in the district attorney's office." Dorcas stood with one hand on her hip, oozing confidence. "Now that all deals are off, I'm going to ask the jury for a ninety-nine-year sentence." She gave Camille a tight little smile. "I'd like to see Jenny's face when you tell her that. It ought to give her something to chew on." She hurried away before Camille could answer. *Ninety-nine years?* Camille's heart fell. No matter how hard she tried to protect her client, the situation kept getting worse. Dorcas was steadily tightening the screws. Camille tossed aside her legal tablet in disgust. Yes, Dorcas would do it. She'd ask the jury for a maximum sentence. Just to get across the message that it didn't pay to defy the prosecutor.

Camille glanced around the empty courtroom. In one short hour the system would crank into operation, and before it was over, Jenny might be diced, shredded and packaged. There was only one thing standing between Jenny and a ninety-nine year-sentence, and that was Camille's skill as a trial lawyer. She lowered her head to her palms and experienced the enormous weight of her responsibility. She had virtually nothing to offer in Jenny's defense, yet the girl's fate rested in Camille's inadequate hands. Was Jenny doomed? Was there nothing Camille could do to rescue her?

Camille got up and paced the courtroom, struggling in vain for an answer. The only thought that came to mind was the almost-forgotten advice of her friend Geoff Vance. Throw up a smoke screen. Divert attention from Jenny by attacking Pike. At first Camille shrank from the notion, desperately seeking another option. There had to be another way. She didn't want to be like Dorcas, using people and bullying them for some ulterior motive, experiencing no sense of guilt because of a warped personal philosophy that the ends justify the means. But where was the justice in imposing a ninety-nine-year prison sentence on a seventeen-year-old girl, just because that girl was terrified of Weasel Robertson and refused the prosecutor's "sweet deal"?

Red-hot anger flared in Camille. Dorcas hadn't played fair. And Pike was part of the whole rotten scheme. He was the one who wanted Weasel Robertson. *Pike wants Weasel, but he doesn't want you,* mocked her heart. Pike was cold and unfeeling, spurning the love she'd offered so freely just as he spurned the possibility of rehabilitating a young girl like Jenny. He cared about nothing but arrests and convictions. If Camille could tear him apart on the witness stand, it was no more than he deserved. And if she succeeded, it would be sweet revenge for the unmitigated hell he'd put her through. She owed him plenty. It would be a pleasure to watch him suffer. Fate had put the weapon in Camille's hands, and she would use it.

She went back to the counsel table and grabbed her legal tablet. She would cross-examine him about his wife's death in an armed robbery and the guilt he must've had ever since because he hadn't been able to save her life. She'd force him to testify about his single-minded dedication to police work ever since and his bitterness about violent crimes. Yes, it should work. Jenny looked so young and helpless that the jury would give her the benefit of every doubt. Camille shuddered, then scribbled a few questions on her tablet:

Why didn't you do anything to save your wife when the robber took her hostage?

You still feel guilty, don't you?

You're still trying to make up for your failure by convicting other people, aren't you?

You're especially bitter toward Jenny because she refused to put the blame on someone you wanted to catch, aren't you?

Tears filled Camille's eyes, but she angrily shook them away. She'd just made the most gut-wrenching choice of her life—Pike or Jenny? She really had no choice. She had to defend her client to the best of her ability. Pike's rejection had finally made her tough enough to do what she must. The page filled with questions that would rip Pike apart.

Pike sat in the witness seat, answering the questions Dorcas asked about his background as a police officer. He'd testified in many trials over the years and didn't have the anxiety of witnesses who were new to the task. He spoke into the microphone and made eye contact with the jury, who listened intently to every word he said. He made a very credible witness, Camille had to admit. He came across as the dogged, determined police officer he was, and probably no one but Camille noticed how careful he was not to look in her direction. She, to the contrary, leaned back and stared at him, hoping to make him a little less sure of himself.

Dorcas started to question him directly about the robbery, and Camille continued to appear unruffled by his answers, even when he made a positive identification of Jenny by pointing her out to the jury as the girl he'd arrested and taken into custody on the night of the robbery.

"There's no doubt in your mind that Jenny Mayner is the person you saw with a gun pointed at the store clerk?" asked Dorcas.

"No, ma'am. I'd seen her before when I was assigned to the East Austin beat, and I recognized her at the time of the holdup." His voice was deep and self-assured.

"Where were you when you first realized a robbery was taking place?"

"I was in a squad car, training a rookie police officer. We could see through the store's display window as we drove through the parking lot. The clerk inside had his hands in the air, and the defendant was waving a gun like it was too heavy for her to hold straight. We parked the squad car, radioed for a backup unit, and went inside with our guns drawn."

"What did Jenny Mayner do then?"

"She kind of fell apart, I guess. Just slumped to the floor with the gun in her hand. It was almost like she was glad she'd been caught, or relieved that she hadn't gone through with the robbery."

Camille was surprised at his answer, since it was helpful to Jenny. There had been nothing in the offense report about Jenny's emotional condition at the time of her arrest, so this was the first time Camille knew about it. Pike was going to play fair, after all, and tell it the way it happened, even when he didn't have to. She had to give him her begrudging admiration. He was going to catch hell from Dorcas later, though. Dorcas was already trying to minimize the effect of his answer with another question.

"Did you notice the victim's condition at the time you entered the building?" she asked. "Did he think it was only a joke, or was he frightened?"

"He was afraid, all right. There was sweat running down his forehead."

Dorcas reached into an evidence bag and pulled out a gun in a plastic bag. "May I approach the witness, your Honor?" she asked the judge. It was impermissible for an attorney to leave the counsel table when a witness was testifying unless the judge granted permission. The rule was to protect witnesses from over-enthusiastic lawyers who might otherwise get in their faces and shout their questions, either to intimidate them or for dramatic effect with the jury. The judge nodded at Dorcas, who carried the plastic bag to the front of the courtroom and handed it to Pike. "Do you recognize this gun?" she asked.

"Yes, ma'am. It's sealed and taped, with my initials marking the date and time I received it. I took it from Jenny Mayner at the scene of the crime. She dropped it into this plastic evidence bag with her own hands."

"Is it a real gun, Lieutenant Barrett?"

"Oh, yes, ma'am."

"So the victim was entitled to be afraid when the defendant threatened him with it? It's enough to make anybody sweat to look down the barrel of something like this?"

Camille stood. "Objection, your Honor. The prosecutor is leading the witness."

"Objection sustained. Rephrase your question, counsel, and let the witness answer in his own words."

"I'll withdraw the question, your Honor."

Not that it matters, Camille thought. Dorcas had already made her point with the jury. They wouldn't think of that gun again without remembering the store clerk sweating with fear.

Dorcas went through all the questions she had to ask to prove her case, including the chain of custody of the gun. Pike testified to turning in the plastic bag to the evidence officer at the police station. Later the evidence officer would take the stand to explain to the jury that the gun had been in police custody ever since. Pike himself had checked it out this morning and brought it to the courtroom and handed it to Dorcas

Wilson. He even showed the markings on the label where this information was recorded.

The testimony was fairly tedious, and the jury began to get restless. Camille had noticed before that juries always expect a courtroom trial to be dramatic, the way it is on television. In real life, however, the questions tended to be dull, the answers more so, and the witnesses nondescript. This jury was luckier than most. The testimony might be dull, but Pike himself projected energy and charisma. Camille wished she had better control of her emotions. She found herself hanging on to Pike's every word, and not entirely on Jenny's account.

"Your witness, counsel," Dorcas said. She'd made her points with the jury. Nobody in the room had a single doubt that Jenny Mayner was guilty as charged.

Camille drew a deep breath, then looked down at her yellow legal tablet with the questions that would undermine Pike's testimony. *Not yet,* she thought. *Soften him up a little first, then move in for the kill.* She asked the first question that popped into her head.

"Lieutenant Barrett, you told the prosecutor that you recognized Jenny Mayner from previous experience as a cop who covered her neighborhood beat. Do you know her family?"

"I know who they are. She has a mother and a younger sister."

"No father?"

"Her parents were divorced a long time ago. Her father left town, and as far as I know, never came back."

"Do you see her mother and sister in the courtroom today?"

"No, they're not here."

"Is anybody here to give Jenny Mayner moral support while she's on trial and facing a long prison sentence for armed robbery?"

Camille watched the jury turn to look at the empty pews in the courtroom. No one was there except the bailiff.

"No, ma'am."

"Doesn't that strike you as a little bit odd, Lieutenant? For a young girl to face this court proceeding all by herself?"

Camille could feel Jenny's hand gripping her elbow. *Dear God, no,* she prayed. *Keep her quiet until I'm through.*

Dorcas was on her feet. "Objection, your Honor. This is irrelevant. Whether the defendant has family in the courtroom has nothing to do with her guilt on an armed robbery charge."

Before the judge could rule on Dorcas's motion, Camille was on her feet. "May we approach the bench, your Honor?" Hurrying forward with Dorcas at his nod, she whispered so the jury couldn't hear. "Your Honor, this line of questioning has to do with mitigating circumstances. It will also affect the punishment phase of the trial. Please let me continue. I'll show the relevance of the questions."

Even as she spoke, Camille was amazed at herself. The words were coming from some deep, instinctive part of her that was far beyond the reach of her rational mind. *Gut instinct,* that's what it was. She'd never experienced it before, but she'd heard other lawyers talk about it.

"I'm going to allow this one question," the judge said. "Then I want you to move on to something else."

"Yes, your Honor." She returned to her seat and turned to face Pike again. "Do you want the question repeated?" she asked.

"No, ma'am. You asked why Jenny Mayner is in court all by herself, with no family for moral support. It's because her mother has never been able to cope with life since her husband went south. She still lives in the same house with her children, but she's abandoned them. She did that a long time ago. And she's been sliding down the path of least resistance ever since."

Camille could feel the rising agitation in Jenny beside her. She reached out to take Jenny's wrist and gripped it so hard it must have hurt. "Not one word," she whispered with all the strength she could muster. "You know he's telling the truth, and I need it to save your skin."

Jenny's wrist went limp in her hand, and Camille chanced a quick glance at the girl's face. It was pale, very pale, and tears were running down her cheeks and falling onto her blouse. Camille fumbled in her purse for a handful of tissue and handed it to Jenny. ''Blow.''

Camille turned her attention back to Pike. She could almost feel the animosity he was directing toward her. But why? *He* was the one who'd walked out on *her*. She was the one with a right to be indignant. She was the one who should be able to cut him into slivers and laugh about doing it. She was the one with the weapon to destroy him, and destroy him she would. She picked up her tablet.

Their glances met. He sat there in the witness seat, so tall the microphone had to be tilted upward for him. He wore a dark tweed jacket and navy slacks, looking for all the world like a simple, sincere cop who was just trying to do his job. There was no doubt about it, though, he was angry with her. He didn't like the questions she was asking him on cross-examination, but there was something deeper than anger. He was hurt. Camille gave him another careful look. Hurt? Pike Barrett, the man with asbestos in place of emotions? It didn't make sense. Why was he staring at her with that expression of wounded betrayal? Were his own instincts working overtime, warning him that Camille intended to do just that, betray him by invading his privacy in front of this jury, poking at his secret scars and mocking his pain?

Camille laid her tablet on the desk. Where was the justice she claimed to value more than life itself if the only way to help one person was to destroy another? God help her, she couldn't do it. She wasn't tough enough. She would have to find another way.

There was a catch in her voice, but she spoke loudly enough for the court reporter to hear. "No more questions. This witness may be excused."

Chapter Twelve

Jenny, I think you need to take the witness stand and let the jury get to know you," Camille said during the late-afternoon break in the trial. Dorcas had finished putting on the State's case sooner than anticipated, and after the recess it would be Camille's turn. "I've done everything I can with the State's witnesses, and now the jury wants to hear from you."

Jenny shook her head. "I'm scared," she said, hardly able to make a sound.

"Of course you are. Anybody would be scared in these circumstances." Camille stood and shoved her hands into the pockets of her gray plaid jacket. It was always difficult to decide whether to have a defendant take the stand. If the jury took a dislike to the person, they would impose a more severe sentence. "It's a risk, Jenny. It could backfire on us. But the jury has sat there all afternoon listening to the police officers describe what happened during the robbery. They've looked at you and tried to imagine you in that store with a gun. They have a lot of questions about what kind of person you are."

"What if I don't testify? What's going to happen?"

"The judge will instruct the jury that they can't hold it against you because you didn't testify in your own behalf. He'll tell them you have a constitutional right to remain silent."

"Sure, just like on TV. So they'll know I'm guilty anyway." Jenny got up from the counsel table and walked over to the windows along one wall. "There's a dog down there with his leg hiked at a parking meter," she said, uttering a dry laugh. "Do you know what it's like to be locked up where you can't see the sky or the trees or the grass? I never thought it would give me such a kick to see a spotted dog with his foot in the air." She watched for a few minutes longer, then walked back over to the counsel table. "I don't know what to do," she said, flinging herself onto a chair.

"The decision is yours, Jenny. I'm going to do the best I can for you, whatever you decide."

"Yeah." Jenny sighed. "Okay. I'll do it. They can't do worse than give me ninety-nine years, right?"

The jury filed back into the courtroom, accompanied by the bailiff. Dorcas hurried in at the last minute, leaving her witnesses to wait in the corridor outside the courtroom. Camille knew Pike was out there somewhere, probably fidgeting at the forced inactivity. That was part of the process, long hours sitting on the bench because witnesses couldn't leave the courthouse in case they were needed for rebuttal later, but they couldn't come inside the courtroom and hear what other witnesses were saying. For the lawyer concerned with questioning witnesses and introducing exhibits, the time in the courtroom passed all too quickly. For everybody else, a trial seemed interminable.

Everybody stood as the judge entered the courtroom. "Is the defense ready to proceed?" he asked, when everybody had been seated again.

"Yes, your Honor. The defense calls Jenny Mayner."

Camille noted the jury's interest as Jenny left the counsel table and went to the witness stand. Her taffy-colored hair hung loose down her back, and with the weight she'd lost in jail, she looked frail. Her voice quavered as the clerk administered the oath. At the moment she looked and sounded like a twelve-year-old. If only she could hold herself together for a little while longer...

"Jenny, you've been in the courtroom throughout the trial and heard the testimony of all the other witnesses, isn't that correct?" Camille asked.

Jenny nodded.

"You'll have to speak up," the judge said. "The court reporter needs to record your answer."

"Yes," Jenny answered in a high, thin voice. "I've heard them."

"You've heard them describe an attempted armed robbery on the night of November sixth?"

"Yes." Jenny's eyes were fixed on her hands, clenched in her lap.

"Now, before we get into that, I'd like for you to tell the jury a little bit about yourself, okay?" Camille was doing her best to set Jenny at ease and let her get comfortable in the witness box before they got into the difficulties of explaining the robbery. "How old are you, Jenny?"

"Seventeen."

"And do you attend school?"

"Yes. Well, I did, until I went to jail. I'm a junior."

"What kind of grades do you make?"

"I've been doing real good the past two years. I've been on the honor roll every time." Jenny looked up but didn't seem to see the courtroom. Instead she seemed to be watching her future disappear before her very eyes. "I hoped I might get a scholarship," she said wistfully. "Go to college. Everybody else in our family has always dropped out of school. For a little while I thought I could be different."

"What did you want to study in college?" Camille asked. This was a learning experience for her as well as for the jury. Jenny had been so uncommunicative that Camille knew very little about her dreams and aspirations.

"I thought I'd like to be a physical therapist, you know? Help people who'd been hurt. Maybe teach them to walk again and things like that."

"What else did you do besides go to school?" Camille asked. She was pleased with Jenny's responses. The jury was listening intently and seemed impressed.

"I had a job after school. At first I worked at McDonald's, but then I got a job at a restaurant over by our house. I could make tips there, and they'd usually give me leftover food to take home."

"What did you do with your salary?" Camille asked. "Buy clothes and stereo equipment the way most teenagers do?"

Dorcas stood and interrupted before Jenny could answer. "Objection, your Honor. I've tried to be patient, but counsel is leading the witness and these questions are irrelevant."

Camille opened her mouth to respond, but it wasn't necessary.

"I'll allow the question," Judge Michelsohn said. "Try not to lead your witness, counsel."

"Thank you, your Honor." Camille gave Jenny an encouraging smile. "How did you spend your salary?"

"Mostly it went for the rent. If there was anything left over, I might take my little sister to the dollar movie."

Camille knew she had to proceed cautiously now. Jenny always blew up when there was any kind of criticism of her mother. "Have you pretty much had the responsibility to support your family?" she asked.

Jenny glanced away, toward the jury. She seemed to want to clear up any misconception they might have about her family. "My mom's not really able to work, you know? She's never been trained to do anything so it's been real hard for her to get a job. She used to work at a bar sometimes, but I couldn't let her do that anymore. She was real pretty. It wasn't good for her, all those drunks and bad guys hanging around her all the time." Jenny struggled for words. "So she tried some other job, working in a laundry and stuff like that. But they always put so much pressure on her she couldn't handle it. She's not really sick, but she's not strong like other people. She can't take a lot of pressure." She lifted her hands and shrugged. "I guess that's it. I was glad when I got old enough to go to work and help out."

"So your family had a pretty hard time financially?" Camille asked.

"Yeah."

"And you figured it was up to you to provide for your family?"

"Yes, I guess so." Jenny was getting cautious, now. She'd done what she wanted to do in defending her family, but she seemed confused that the questions continued.

"You were needing money for them on the night of the robbery?" Camille held her breath, waiting for Jenny's response. It was a risk to ask the question, but she had to try to establish a motive for Jenny's actions that night.

"What are you talking about?" Jenny's fingers gripped the arms of the witness chair. "Do you want them to believe I did it because we needed money?" An angry crimson stained her cheeks, in stark contrast to her jail house pallor. "I worked and made a living for us. I'm not a thief, Camille. I didn't steal to support my family."

Jenny blurted out her answer before she realized the implications of it.

"Then why did you hold up the clerk in that store?" Camille demanded.

Jenny sat in silent rage.

"You don't deny you're the one who did it?"

Again there was silence.

Camille lowered her voice to a mere whisper, so soft everyone in the room had to strain to hear her. "Did someone force you to hold up that store?" she asked.

Jenny crossed her arms across her chest and stared angrily out the window.

The silence was broken by the judge's voice. "I'm going to instruct you to answer your attorney's question. Did someone force you to commit an armed robbery?"

Jenny whirled in her seat, turning her back on the judge.

"Miss Mayner, you must answer the question," he insisted.

"No!"

He tried to be kind. "If someone forced you to commit a crime," he explained, "then you have a defense for your actions. We call that the defense of 'duress.' The jury must know whether you were forced to commit a crime against your will. Please answer the question."

Jenny burst into tears. "You did this on purpose!" she shouted at Camille. "You got me up here so you could trick me. You're just like all the others!" She doubled up in the chair, her head in her lap, crying hysterically.

The jury watched the unraveling of the drama in astonishment. The bailiff hurried from his post at the courtroom door to the witness seat with a glass of water, but Jenny knocked it from his hand. He stepped back and left her shrunken in the corner of the seat, weeping.

"I'm going to recess this trial until tomorrow morning," the judge said. "Bailiff, will you take the jury from the courtroom. I want to have a word with the attorneys."

The jury obviously didn't want to leave at this point, and watched over their shoulders as they filed from the courtroom. As soon as the door closed behind them, leaving the courtroom empty except for the lawyers and the defendant, the judge spoke again.

"I'll entertain motions for a mistrial tomorrow morning at eight o'clock. Brief the issue, will you, and bring copies of any cases you find. I'm not sure what the law books say about a situation like this."

Dorcas was taking great delight in this unexpected turn of events. "I don't believe the State will ask for a mistrial, your Honor. The defendant took the stand of her own free will. If her actions prejudiced the jury against her, well, that's the risk any defendant takes."

"Miss Clark?"

Camille was worried about Jenny. She was still huddled in a ball in the witness seat, crying. "I'll need to talk to my client," she said.

The judge looked at Jenny, then turned to the bailiff, who was just returning. "Get a matron to take the defendant back to the jail and see if she needs a doctor. Miss Mayner, are you listening to me? Your lawyer needs to talk to you, but she's going to wait until later, when you've had time to get yourself under control again. The bailiff is going to take you back to the jail now."

Jenny was surprisingly docile when the bailiff put the handcuffs on her and helped her down from the witness stand. The fight had gone out of her, but not the anger. She refused to look in Camille's direction as she left the room.

"Whew!" uttered the judge. "What an afternoon." With a grin at the court reporter, he added, "That groan was off the record, Marcia." He stood and stretched to relieve his kinked muscles. "Court stands in recess until eight o'clock tomorrow morning."

Camille sat at her kitchen table with papers and copies of court cases in a dozen different stacks. It was so hard to know how to proceed next with a volatile client like Jenny Mayner. As Camille went over the day's events in her mind, it seemed that things weren't nearly so disastrous as they'd appeared to be at the time. For one thing, Jenny had been totally credible as the overly protective daughter who'd taken it upon herself to support her family. For another, Pike Barrett himself had supported the conclusion that Lois Mayner was an irresponsible parent.

And Jenny's outburst had certainly planted the idea that something unusual lay behind the robbery. Dorcas's fingerprint expert had testified that one print on the gun was made by Weasel Robertson. In closing argument, Camille could draw a connection between Weasel's fingerprint and Jenny's hysterical reaction to a question about whether she'd been forced to commit the robbery. If she got to make a closing argument . . . if the judge didn't declare a mistrial the first thing in the morning . . .

Camille read through the cases in her stack again. She'd run by her office to do some quick research in the law library, and while Alice Gordon had photocopied the cases for her, Camille went to the jail to see Jenny. It had been a waste of time, though. The guard told her that Jenny had called her mother as soon as she returned from the courthouse, and then the doctor had come and decided she needed a mild sedative. The doctor left instructions not to waken her, so it would be morning before Camille could talk to her.

She got up and poured herself a diet cola, too restless to settle down. The trial had put her on edge, and even though she hoped Jenny's position was better at the end of the day than it had been at the beginning, she wasn't sure. Would it have changed anything if she hadn't lost her nerve and attacked Pike's credibility? She'd had him in her hands. All she had to do was squeeze. And she hadn't done it.

She still wasn't exactly sure why not. At the time she'd thought it was because she wasn't tough enough, but tonight that answer seemed too simplistic. She had also been true to herself, to her own integrity. For the first time since her divorce she'd quit playing a role and done what she believed was right instead of doing what would make her look strong in the eyes of other people. But had it cost her the trial? It was too soon to know.

The doorbell rang as she was sipping her drink. She went to answer it in jeans and a sweatshirt, tugging on her sneakers as she crossed the living room.

"Oh," she said, too surprised to say anything else.

"Can I come in?" Pike asked. He stood uncertainly, still wearing the tweed jacket and navy slacks he'd worn at the courthouse.

"Sure. Excuse the way I look. I'm working on Jenny's case." Camille stepped out of the way so Pike could come inside. She lifted her shoulders in a shrug. "I'm talking too much."

"Yeah. I drove around the block half a dozen times before I got up the nerve to stop. I figured you'd throw me out."

They exchanged uneasy smiles. Camille was happy to see Pike, despite everything that had happened. Yet she didn't know why he was here, and she was afraid to reveal too much.

"Would you like something to drink?" she asked. "I think there may be some beer in the refrigerator. Or you can have a diet cola." They both knew Pike had been the one to buy the beer, and they were a little embarrassed. That had been in the easy days of their relationship, when they'd made love on the living-room floor during the football games and life was full of joy and promise. That had been two weeks ago, before everything had changed and Camille still didn't understand why.

"I need a beer."

"Sit down and I'll get it for you."

He followed her into the kitchen. "I don't need a glass," he said. "The can is fine."

She reached into the cabinet and pulled down a pilsner glass. "Be my guest." It was one of the little things they'd sparred about before. Already the intimacy they'd shared was seeping into the present moment, reminding them of its power.

Pike sat down at the kitchen table.

"Wouldn't you rather go into the living room?" Camille asked. "I've got my work all over the table."

He shook his head. "I feel more comfortable with a table between us."

Camille pushed some papers out of the way and sat down across from him. He was right. The kitchen was best. The living room held too many memories for both of them.

"I'm sure you didn't drive across town to get a free beer," she said. "What's on your mind, Pike?"

"There's something I've got to find out," he said, studying her carefully. "It's been driving me crazy all day."

Camille pulled her legs underneath her and sat cross-legged on her chair. "What's that?"

"At the trial today, when I was testifying. Why didn't you ask me about my wife?"

"I can't talk to you about the case, Pike. You know the rules. Dorcas isn't here, and she didn't give her permission. Let's talk about something else."

"Dorcas told me you were going to hammer me about that other robbery and my wife being killed. She said you'd carve me up and throw me to the jury. But you didn't do it, Camille. Why?"

"Pike, please, I'm not going to answer your questions. You're still a witness, and the case isn't finished yet. We can't talk about it."

"I saw that look on your face, Camille. You were getting ready to go for blood. And then you stopped, just like that." He snapped his fingers. "Tell me why."

This was too much. Camille knew her own weaknesses, and she didn't need Pike to remind her of them. It couldn't be plainer that he'd seen her lose her nerve. It had been that obvious. "Pike, stop. I'm not going to commit an ethical violation to satisfy your curiosity. When the case is over, we can talk about it. For now, you're going to have to forget it."

"I told Dorcas you wouldn't do it. I told her you weren't like that. But deep down in my heart, I expected the worst and it didn't happen. Why not, Camille?"

"Don't!" Camille cried, rising from her chair. She stood, poised for a moment like a bird in midflight, motionless.

A shot rang out, and a bullet shattered the kitchen window before it smashed into the opposite wall.

Pike's hand flew out and shoved Camille to the floor. "Stay down!" He flipped off the light, then dropped onto the floor beside her. "Are you okay?" he asked, grappling for her in the darkness.

Her teeth were chattering too hard for her to talk. She huddled in a ball, and when Pike's arms came around her, she buried her head in his shoulder, her whole body now shaking with paroxysms of fear.

He hugged her tight for a moment, then drew his gun. "I'll be right back," he promised. He reached above his head until he found the doorknob, then silently opened the door.

"Pike, don't go out there," she cried. "You'll get yourself killed."

"Shh." With that, he was gone. There wasn't even the comfort of the sound of his breathing. Camille curled into a knot and crouched under the kitchen table, imagining the worst. Outside she could hear shouts, then the sound of more gunfire. Dear God, what if he got killed? She began to weep. How could she live without him? She loved him so much. She rocked back and forth in pain. *Please, please, let him be safe.* She wouldn't ask anything else, if he could just be protected. "Pike, Pike..." she said over and over, repeating his name like a prayer.

* * *

"Camille, it's all over," he said as he opened the kitchen door a good ten minutes later. The light flashed on, and he scooped her into his arms. "It was Weasel Robertson," he said, kissing her, smoothing his hand over her worried face, soothing her quivering body. "We had him under surveillance, but the detail lost him for a few blocks. I'm going to roast their hides and make them wish they were safe in jail themselves." He hugged Camille so tightly she could scarcely breathe. "They lost him for a few blocks and you nearly got killed because of it."

"Why was Weasel shooting at me?" Camille asked. The whole thing had happened so fast her head was spinning.

"Who knows? My guess is you got too close to him. I gave him his *Miranda* warnings and he said he wants a lawyer. I can't ask him any questions." He kissed Camille's lips hard and fast. "I've got to take him to the station and book him. I'm having a detail watch your house for the rest of the night, just in case Weasel has some friends around to finish the job."

"Thanks," she said, snuggling against him for one last time. "I'll feel safer with someone out there tonight."

"You're not going to be here," Pike said. "One of the guys will take you to my place for the rest of the night. There'll be a detail there, too, because I'll be at the station for hours. I'm not leaving you unprotected."

"But, Pike, that's unnecessary. I'll be fine here. Honest. What more could I ask? You've left me well protected."

"Will you please quit arguing," he muttered. "You're not as tough as you'd like everybody to think you are. I want to be sure you live to see Jenny's trial finished."

Gary Fletcher was the only officer in the special crimes unit when Pike went in to fill out his reports.

"So you finally got Weasel Robertson?" Gary asked. "Way to go, man."

"Attempted homicide. That ought to put him away for a while."

"You don't sound too happy about it."

Pike had been distracted with the reports, but he looked up. "I'm happy. Happy we caught him, anyway. Not too happy with his choice of victim. I don't think he missed Camille Clark by half an inch."

"Oh, yeah? Camille Clark, huh?"

Pike didn't like the knowing expression on his buddy's face. "Take a hike, Fletcher."

"I didn't say a word."

"You didn't have to. Make yourself useful and bring me a cup of coffee, will you?"

Gary brought two steaming cups of coffee, one of them well-laced with cream and sugar. "Thought I'd join you." He sat down at the desk and read over Pike's shoulder. "So is this thing with Camille Clark serious?" he asked.

"Fletcher, you know I don't talk about my personal business at work. Never have, never will."

"Yeah, yeah. Well, suit yourself. Everybody figures you're a goner this time anyway. If she'll have you."

"If *she* will have *me*?"

"Right. She's supposed to be pretty bright, though. She may have better sense. Especially if some of us who know you clue her in on your shortcomings."

"Like what?" Pike took a big gulp of scalding coffee, then wished he hadn't.

"Don't believe I'll say. I don't want to find myself horseback on Sixth Street directing traffic on Saturday nights." He gave a hearty laugh. "See you tomorrow, boss. I'm out of here."

Pike settled back in his chair. He was comfortable at the station. He'd spent the biggest part of his life here. It was his world, and he was in control. Over the years he'd lost his identity in his work. The attempt on Camille's life tonight had shattered all that. There was a reality beyond the four walls of the police station, and Camille had lured him away from his comfortable cocoon. If he let her into his heart and life, he would become vulnerable again, the way he'd been with Annie. He'd steered clear of involvement all these years because he didn't want to relive that. Was he willing now to pay the price?

Part of him said no. He wanted to keep himself closed off, crawl back into his cocoon where he'd be safe. But at what cost? What would he be giving up? After knowing Camille, could he settle for another kind of woman, one who would demand less from him and give less of herself? There were women like that, and he'd deliberately chosen them in the past. They'd satisfied his body, but they'd never satisfied his heart. Only Camille, with her warmth that gave, seeking nothing in return, could do that.

He crossed his hands behind his head and leaned back in his chair. Camille. What made her tick? Why hadn't she taken advantage of him today and cross-examined him about his past?

If he knew the answer to that question, he'd know the secret to what was in her heart. And until the trial was over, he wasn't going to get an answer.

Chapter Thirteen

The clock's hands stood at eight o'clock sharp when a guard hurried into the courtroom with Jenny Mayner the following morning. Camille was already at the counsel table, as was Dorcas Wilson. The courtroom bailiff had the jury panel lined up ready to march inside. The judge was standing at the door connecting his chambers to the courtroom. It was time for court to begin.

The guard unlocked Jenny's handcuffs, and she sat down without acknowledging Camille's presence. She was obviously still upset, and everything had conspired to keep Camille from having an opportunity to talk to her.

"Jenny, I came to the jail to see you early this morning," Camille tried to explain. "They said they had doctor's orders not to wake you up."

"Leave me alone, Camille. Let's get this over with."

"You don't understand," Camille said, reaching for Jenny's hand. She only meant to reassure her client, but Jenny jerked away from the contact. Camille turned to the guard. "Ask the judge if he'll give me a few minutes alone with my client before we begin."

"No, no more talk." Jenny was adamant.

It was too late. "All rise," called the bailiff, and the jury panel filed in.

The judge entered through his private doorway. "Be seated. Do the attorneys have any motions to present to the court?"

Camille turned to Jenny with an urgent whisper. "Jenny, this is the time for me to ask for a mistrial. If the judge grants my motion, we can start over with a new trial later on."

"No. Get it over with. I don't want another trial."

"At least let me ask for a conference so we can talk about it."

Jenny's expression was sullen but determined. "There's nothing to talk about."

"Yes, I need to talk to you about Weasel Robertson—"

Jenny's lips clenched tight.

"Will counsel approach the bench?" requested the judge. Camille and Dorcas headed for the bench, and the court reporter joined the huddle so everything they said would be recorded.

"Do either of you intend to ask for a mistrial?" Judge Michelsohn asked, speaking low so the jury couldn't hear.

"No, the State does not." Dorcas seemed to be quite pleased with the way the case was going.

Camille had to ask for a conference with Jenny, even though Jenny didn't want one. "Judge, my client was just brought in from the jail. She says she doesn't want to ask for a mistrial, but I haven't had a chance to explain things to her. Could you indulge me by giving me time for a brief conference?"

The judge looked across at Jenny. She was sitting morosely at the counsel table. "I don't want to do anything that's going to deny your client's rights, but I also don't want her to get upset in front of the jury," he said. "Do *you* want to request a mistrial?"

"I spent hours reading the cases last night," Camille answered. "I'm going to recommend that we go forward and finish this trial."

"I'll send the jury out for fifteen minutes. We'll clear the courtroom and you can talk to your client at the counsel table. If there's the slightest hint she's going to have another outburst, I'm going to declare a mistrial on my own motion."

"Jenny, listen to me," Camille said when everyone was gone. "I agree that we shouldn't request a mistrial, but I want to be sure you understand the consequences. Another jury might let you off scot-free.''

"I'm *never* going through this again. I was stupid to listen to you and have a trial in the first place. I won't do it again.'' She edged away from Camille. The anger was still there, but the sedative had tempered it. At least she wasn't yelling. Camille could scarcely look at Jenny without tears springing to her lashes, though. Even in her high-school skirt and sweater, Jenny looked old and tired and defeated. She was a seventeen-year-old version of Lois Mayner.

"Okay, I'll tell the judge that we agree not to request a mistrial.'' Camille glanced at the clock. They were almost out of time. "I have to tell you about Weasel Robertson. He was arrested last night.''

Jenny gasped. "Arrested? What for?''

"Attempted homicide.'' This was no time to give Jenny the gory details and distract her attention from the trial. Camille still hoped to win some sympathy for her client. "He's going to be locked up for a long, long time. You don't have to be afraid of him anymore, Jenny.''

Jenny buried her face in her hands. "I can't believe it,'' she whispered over and over.

"It's true. You don't have to be afraid to testify against him now.''

There was a noise at the courtroom door, and they turned to see whether the jury was being brought in. Instead it was Lois Mayner with Sylvia, arguing with the bailiff who'd been given instructions to keep the courtroom clear.

"Mom," Jenny said, hurrying over, Camille right behind her. "I told you not to come." She reached out and hugged Sylvia, and when she pulled away, tears were trickling down her cheeks. "I've missed you," she said.

"After you called me last night, I knew I had to come," Lois said. Her lip was trembling, but her head was higher than Camille had ever seen it. "No matter what Weasel said, you're my baby. You needed me. I told him I was coming down here whether he liked it or not."

"Mom, Camille just told me that Weasel's in jail. Did you know that?"

Lois could only shake her head, too surprised to speak.

There was no more time to talk. The bailiff took his responsibilities seriously, and Lois and Sylvia were taken outside until the jury was seated again and the judge was on the bench. The trial was continuing where it left off, with Jenny on the witness stand, when the Mayners slipped quietly into a side pew to give her their love and moral support.

Even before it became visible, Camille sensed that the tide of the trial had turned in Jenny's direction. In one part of her mind, Camille remembered how carefully she'd dressed this morning, choosing a black wool jacket with big shoulder pads and a slim black-

and-white houndstooth check skirt. As though it
mattered what she wore into the courtroom. How superficial she'd been! What mattered was the truth.
That alone was the real source of power and justice.
And now Jenny Mayner was going to tell the truth, the
whole truth, and nothing but the truth, so help her
God.

"Yesterday you became very upset when I asked
you whether anyone had forced you to commit this
armed robbery. Will you tell the jury why?" asked
Camille.

"Because I was afraid."

"Who were you afraid of?"

"Weasel Robertson."

"Is he the person whose fingerprint was on the gun
you used in the armed robbery?"

"Yes."

"Did you get the gun from him?"

"Yes."

Camille had to feel her way. She was in uncharted
territory, and that could be dangerous. Trial lawyers
learn from the beginning of their training never to ask
a question unless they know what the answer will be.
And Camille didn't know the answers this time. Jenny
had never told her. She was going to have to play her
hunches.

"Why aren't you afraid now?" she asked.

"Because you told me he was arrested last night. If
he's locked up, he can't hurt us."

"Us?"

Jenny's hands twisted in her lap. "My family. My mom and little sister."

Dorcas stood to make an objection. "Your Honor, this testimony is improper. It has nothing to do with the criminal offense this defendant is charged with committing."

Camille stood to respond. The testimony was highly relevant, and she felt sure the judge would overrule Dorcas's objection. The interruption had simply been a trial tactic to distract the jury and thereby minimize the effect of Jenny's testimony. It was an old trick, but irritating nevertheless. "Your Honor, this testimony goes to the defense of duress," she said. "I'm establishing the defendant's motive for committing the crime."

"Objection overruled. You may proceed."

"How did you come to know a man like Weasel Robertson?" Camille asked Jenny.

"He used to be my mom's boyfriend. He left for a couple of years, but then he came back."

From the corner of her eye, Camille could see the jury lean forward to listen. "And that's when he somehow did something to make you afraid of him?"

Jenny's face was stricken. "It started before. The first time he was here."

"What did he do, Jenny?" All at once Camille thought she knew what had happened. She could almost feel the answer in her bones. Why hadn't she had sense enough to realize? The pattern was there, all of it. All those runaway offenses when Jenny was four-teen and fifteen, trying to escape an intolerable situa-tion at home.

"I—he—" Jenny flushed. "I don't want to talk about it."

"Did your mother know about it, Jenny? Did your mother know he sexually abused you?"

"No. I couldn't tell her. She thought he was great because he gave her money when she needed it. She didn't know what he was really like. Mom's a good person herself, and she believes everybody else is, too."

To the end, Jenny would stand up for her mother. Camille swallowed hard. It was so much more than Lois Mayner deserved.

She turned to see what effect Jenny's testimony was having on Lois. Tears, as she expected. As though crying could change anything! But maybe things would be different now. For Sylvia's sake, Camille hoped so. She was a beautiful little girl. It would be a shame if her life was ruined as Jenny's had been.

"After Weasel left town, that's when you got a job and started doing well in school?"

"Yes. For two years." Jenny didn't cry, but the pain in her voice expressed her sense of loss. For two years she'd had hope, and then it was snatched away from her.

"Then Weasel came back, and it started all over again?"

Jenny shook her head. "No. I was older and bigger. I told him I'd kill him if he touched me again. He knew I meant it."

This didn't make sense. Camille had to clear it up for the jury. How could they believe she was too frightened to testify about Weasel when she'd apparently been quite able to protect herself? "Then how did he force you to rob that store? He wasn't anywhere near when the robbery occurred."

"He needed the money. He said I had to do it or else."

Camille had to ask the question without knowing what the answer was going to be. It was against all the rules of litigation.

Camille took a deep breath. "Or else what, Jenny?"

"Or else he was going to do worse things to Sylvia than he'd done to me." She lowered her face into her hands and began to weep.

The jurors turned to one another and gave in to the urge to exclaim over what had happened. The judge had to bang his gavel to bring order into the courtroom again.

When the room was quiet, Jenny turned to face the judge. Choking on her tears, she said, "It was stupid of me to try to handle it myself. I should've gone to the police. I was too scared to think straight." Then she turned to the jury. "I was so glad when the cops came into that store and arrested me. It was a relief to get caught and not have to go through with it."

Camille didn't even bother to go back to her office when the trial ended. She headed straight home, knowing somehow that Pike would be there soon. She hadn't been able to talk to him at the courthouse because of all the pandemonium that broke out. Television reporters had gotten wind of a human-interest story that would play well on the six o'clock news, and they'd swarmed the corridors getting interviews.

She'd changed into a bamboo-colored silk blouse with matching full skirt and a gold serpentine belt. As she fastened a multistrand chain with gold coins around her neck, she decided the shoulder pads in her blouse were too big. Without another thought she snipped the threads and removed the shoulder pads, then tossed them in the wastebasket. She'd learned her lesson. It wasn't the clothes, it was the woman inside who had to be strong.

Camille was through living a lie. There would always be times when she was weak and vulnerable, and that was going to have to be okay. Real strength didn't come from acting tough, it came from being true to her own conscience and to the man she loved. The only problem was that Pike wanted a woman who was tough on the inside as well as the outside. Could he accept her as she was? She didn't know, but it was time to find out.

The doorbell rang, and her stomach flip-flopped. She could hardly wait to tell Pike how much she loved him.

"Hi, sweetheart," he said, kissing her at the door in full view of anybody who cared to watch. "Ummm, you smell good." He kissed her again, then hugged her so hard he nearly squeezed all the breath from her.

"What's that for?" Camille asked, tilting her face for another kiss.

"Because I'm so glad you're still alive." He held her face between the palms of his hands. "I was scared to death last night. I still get the shakes every time I think about what a close call that was."

"Do you want to come see the damage?" she asked. Pike followed her into the kitchen, where the window was boarded up and the shattered glass had been removed. "Those fellows you left here last night were great. They had everything cleaned up when I got home this morning."

Pike tweaked her nose, trying to lighten the intensity of the moment. "I never thought when I finally got you into my bed, I wouldn't be there beside you," he said.

"It's just as well. You'd have been pretty inhibited with two cops in the living room. And Joe Friday."

"Did you sleep okay?"

Camille sighed. "Not really. I had too much on my mind. I spent half the night trying to figure out whether to ask for a mistrial for Jenny."

Pike actually broke into laughter. "You amaze me, you crazy woman. A bullet slams into the wall half an inch from your head, and you spend the night worrying about somebody else's trial." He walked over to the wall where a large hole marked the bullet's final resting place. "Look at that. Thank God it didn't have your name on it."

Camille leaned against his shoulder. She was perfectly capable of standing on her own two feet, but she had to admit it gave her a nice feeling to have someone else worrying about her and feeling protective.

Her arm slipped around Pike's waist. "Want to go into the living room and fool around?" she asked.

"Later. I want to ask you something first."

"Won't it wait?" She turned to face him and slipped her arms around his neck.

He stuck his finger in his collar to loosen it. "First we talk," he said in a strangled voice. When Camille stood on tiptoe and nibbled at his ear, he reached for her hands. "Behave yourself. This is serious."

"It doesn't have to be," she answered. "I know the rules. You told me what you wanted from me. I love you, Pike. I can't help that. But I won't let it be a burden for us."

He gently pushed her onto a kitchen chair and sat down across from her. "Maybe I was wrong. Maybe it's impossible for us to have a relationship that's nothing but easy-loving sex."

"I want you, Pike, whatever the terms. I'll take what I can get because it's better than anything I'm ever going to get from anybody else."

"How do you know that? You haven't even given yourself a chance. Hell, you've only been divorced a year. There are lots of guys out there who can offer you a lot more than I can."

Camille shook her head. "I don't want other guys. I want you."

"But why?"

"Because you're decent and honest and play fair with people."

"How can you say that after the way I stormed out of here on New Year's Eve? I was worse than a jerk, I was a real bastard."

"Yeah, you were. But I think you ran because you'd gotten into more than you'd bargained for. I can forgive you for that."

Pike reached out and clenched her fingers in his hand. "You're the gutsiest woman I've ever met, you know that?"

"Me? I'm made out of marshmallow fluff, or haven't you noticed?"

"Sure I've noticed. I've noticed how you walk straight into Weasel Robertson's apartment and have him hold a knife at your throat without letting that slow you down for a minute. I've noticed how you have a bullet whiz past your ear and all you can think of is how you can try your case. I've noticed how you

hang in there with your client to the bitter end, and
pull off some kind of miracle where she gets off with
five years' probation. I've noticed, all right. And so
has everybody else. The whole courthouse was buzzing when I left there this afternoon. Everyone who gets
arrested is going to be asking you to represent him.''

Camille felt a little embarrassed. "I got some lucky
breaks. Really, it was Jenny's testimony that did it.
She told the truth and the jury believed her. It had
nothing to do with me.''

"Camille, you were court-appointed on that case.
Do you know what anybody else would have done
with a stubborn little tiger like Jenny Mayner? They'd
have let her take that plea bargain for thirty years in
the state penitentiary and never looked back.''

"You act like you don't mind that she got off with
five years' probation. I figured you'd have a fit at the
injustice of it all.''

"The punishment should fit the crime. Besides, I
think you're right. I think Jenny can be rehabilitated.
And it's all because of you.'' There was a tenderness
in Pike's expression that brought tears to Camille's
eyes.

"Don't," she whispered. "Don't have any illusions
about me. I don't want you to think I'm something
I'm not. I can't live a lie anymore. You're going to
have to accept me the way I am, warts and all.''

"Warts? You have warts? Now that, I hadn't noticed.'' He gave her his killer smile. "One more ques-

tion, and then I'm going to start a full-time wart investigation."

"Hurry up, then. Time's awasting, as they say out in the country."

"It's the same question I asked you last night, but you never gave me an answer. Why didn't you tear me apart on cross-examination?"

"Maybe we better have a glass of wine first."

"No wine. Give it to me straight."

Camille sighed. "I meant to, Pike. I thought I had to undermine your testimony, for Jenny's sake. But when it came down to the wire, I couldn't do it. That's what I mean about the marshmallow fluff." She leaned forward and took his hands in hers. "But it was more than that. I've been watching you, too. I know how much integrity you have. I couldn't bring myself to make the jury believe a lie about you. And I couldn't see that there would be any more justice in the world if I sacrificed you to save Jenny. I didn't have that right. A court of law can't be a place of justice unless a trial is based on the truth."

"What if you'd lost the case because you didn't take advantage of that opportunity to rip me into pieces?"

"I did lose the trial," Camille said softly. "Jenny was convicted. She's got to toe the mark the whole time she's on probation. She won't be able to do things other people take for granted, like hop on a plane and go to Dallas for the weekend. She can't make a move without her probation officer's permission. But even if I didn't get an acquittal for her, I didn't lose my self-respect. Winning would be a hollow victory if I'd made the jury believe a lie about you. You're not a Dirty Harry, Pike, no matter how tough you are. You play by the rules and catch the criminals fair and square."

"I tried to push you away," he said. "I didn't want to get involved. I'm not half as tough as you are. I've been too big a coward to take the risk of loving someone again. What you've taught me is that toughness has its place, but not in the heart."

He stood and drew Camille to her feet. "You know what I love about you, sweetheart? Your courage. You're not afraid to give without counting the cost. You loved me when you got nothing in return. And no matter how sorry I treated you, you kept on loving me." His hands tangled in her hair, and he pulled her against his chest. "You just kept on loving me and loving me when I didn't deserve it." His voice broke, and Camille looked up. There were tears in his eyes, threatening to spill loose. He didn't even try to hide them. "I only hope someday I can measure up to you," he whispered. "I'm the luckiest man on earth, Camille."

Their lips met in a long, tender kiss.

"I love you, Pike," Camille murmured.

"I know you do, sweetheart, and that's the wonder of it all." He kissed her again. "I love you, Camille. I love you now, and when the stars turn cold and die,

I'll still be loving you. If you'll have me, I'm yours for now and all eternity.''

Camille gave her answer, not in words, but with the gift of her whole heart and all its love, nothing held back. And somewhere beyond the rainbow, where dreams never die, heaven rejoiced.

*   *   *   *   *

Double your reading pleasure this fall with two Award of Excellence titles written by two of your favorite authors.

Available in September

DUNCAN'S BRIDE
by Linda Howard
Silhouette Intimate Moments #349

Mail-order bride Madelyn Patterson was nothing like what Reese Duncan expected—and everything he needed.

Available in October

THE COWBOY'S LADY
by Debbie Macomber
Silhouette Special Edition #626

The Montana cowboy wanted a little lady at his beck and call—the "lady" in question saw things differently....

These titles have been selected to receive a special laurel—the Award of Excellence. Look for the distinctive emblem on tne cover. It lets you know there's something truly wonderful inside!

DUN-1

**From *New York Times* Bestselling author
Penny Jordan, a compelling novel of ruthless passion
that will mesmerize readers everywhere!**

Penny Jordan

Silver

Real power, true power came from
Rothwell. And Charles vowed to have it,
the earldom and all that went with it.

Silver vowed to destroy Charles, just as surely and
uncaringly as he had destroyed her father; just as he had
intended to destroy her. She needed him to want her . . .
to desire her . . . until he'd do anything to have her.

But first she needed a tutor: a man who wanted no one.
He would help her bait the trap.

**Played out on a glittering international stage,
Silver's story leads her from the luxurious comfort of
British aristocracy into the depths of adventure,
passion and danger.**

AVAILABLE IN OCTOBER!

 **HARLEQUIN**

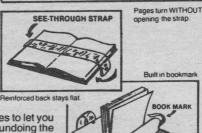

PASSPORT TO ROMANCE VACATION SWEEPSTAKES

OFFICIAL RULES

SWEEPSTAKES RULES AND REGULATIONS. NO PURCHASE NECESSARY.

HOW TO ENTER:

1. To enter, complete this official entry form and return with your invoice in the envelope provided, or print your name, address, telephone number and age on a plain piece of paper and mail to: Passport to Romance, P.O. Box #1397, Buffalo, N.Y. 14269-1397. No mechanically reproduced entries accepted.
2. All entries must be received by the Contest Closing Date, midnight, December 31, 1990 to be eligible.
3. Prizes: There will be ten (10) Grand Prizes awarded, each consisting of a choice of a trip for two people to: i) London, England (approximate retail value $5,050 U.S.); ii) England, Wales and Scotland (approximate retail value $6,400 U.S.); iii) Caribbean Cruise (approximate retail value $7,300 U.S.); iv) Hawaii (approximate retail value $ 9,550 U.S.); v) Greek Island Cruise in the Mediterranean (approximate retail value $12,250 U.S.); vi) France (approximate retail value $7,300 U.S.).
4. Any winner may choose to receive any trip or a cash alternative prize of $5,000.00 U.S. in lieu of the trip.
5. Odds of winning depend on number of entries received.
6. A random draw will be made by Nielsen Promotion Services, an independent judging organization on January 29, 1991, in Buffalo, N.Y., at 11:30 a.m. from all eligible entries received on or before the Contest Closing Date. Any Canadian entrants who are selected must correctly answer a time-limited, mathematical skill-testing question in order to win. Quebec residents may submit any litigation respecting the conduct and awarding of a prize in this contest to the Régie des loteries et courses du Quebec.
7. Full contest rules may be obtained by sending a stamped, self-addressed envelope to: "Passport to Romance Rules Request", P.O. Box 9998, Saint John, New Brunswick, E2L 4N4.
8. Payment of taxes other than air and hotel taxes is the sole responsibility of the winner.
9. Void where prohibited by law.

PASSPORT TO ROMANCE VACATION SWEEPSTAKES

OFFICIAL RULES

SWEEPSTAKES RULES AND REGULATIONS. NO PURCHASE NECESSARY.

HOW TO ENTER:

1. To enter, complete this official entry form and return with your invoice in the envelope provided, or print your name, address, telephone number and age on a plain piece of paper and mail to: Passport to Romance, P.O. Box #1397, Buffalo, N.Y. 14269-1397. No mechanically reproduced entries accepted.
2. All entries must be received by the Contest Closing Date, midnight, December 31, 1990 to be eligible.
3. Prizes: There will be ten (10) Grand Prizes awarded, each consisting of a choice of a trip for two people to: i) London, England (approximate retail value $5,050 U.S.); ii) England, Wales and Scotland (approximate retail value $6,400 U.S.); iii) Caribbean Cruise (approximate retail value $7,300 U.S.); iv) Hawaii (approximate retail value $ 9,550 U.S.); v) Greek Island Cruise in the Mediterranean (approximate retail value $12,250 U.S.); vi) France (approximate retail value $7,300 U.S.).
4. Any winner may choose to receive any trip or a cash alternative prize of $5,000.00 U.S. in lieu of the trip.
5. Odds of winning depend on number of entries received.
6. A random draw will be made by Nielsen Promotion Services, an independent judging organization on January 29, 1991, in Buffalo, N.Y., at 11:30 a.m. from all eligible entries received on or before the Contest Closing Date. Any Canadian entrants who are selected must correctly answer a time-limited, mathematical skill-testing question in order to win. Quebec residents may submit any litigation respecting the conduct and awarding of a prize in this contest to the Régie des loteries et courses du Quebec.
7. Full contest rules may be obtained by sending a stamped, self-addressed envelope to: "Passport to Romance Rules Request", P.O. Box 9998, Saint John, New Brunswick, E2L 4N4.
8. Payment of taxes other than air and hotel taxes is the sole responsibility of the winner.
9. Void where prohibited by law.

© 1990 HARLEQUIN ENTERPRISES LTD.   RLS-DIR